GORE VIDAL wrote his first novel, *Williwaw* (1946), at the age of nineteen while overseas in World War II. During four decades as a writer, Vidal has written novels, plays, short stories, and essays. He has also been a political activist. As a Democratic candidate for Congress from upstate New York, he received the most votes of any Democrat in a half-century. From 1970 to 1972 he was co-chairman of the People's Party. In California's 1982 Democratic primary for U.S. Senate, he polled a half-million votes, and came in second in a field of nine.

In 1948 Vidal wrote the highly praised international best-seller *The City and the Pillar*. This was followed by *The Judgment of Paris* and the prophetic *Messiah*. In the fifties Vidal wrote plays for live television and films for Metro-Goldwyn-Mayer. One of the television plays became the successful Broadway play *Visit to a Small Planet* (1957). Directly for the theater he wrote the prize-winning hit *The Best Man* (1960). In 1964 Vidal returned to the novel with *Julian*, the story of the apostate Roman emperor. This novel has been published in many languages and editions. As Henry de Montherlant wrote: "*Julian is* the only book about a Roman emperor that I like to re-read. Vidal loves his protagonist; he knows the period thoroughly; and the book is a beautiful hymn to the twilight of paganism." During the last quarter-century Vidal has been telling the history of the United States as experienced by one family and its connections in what Gabriel García Márquez has called "Gore Vidal's magnificent series of historical novels or novelized histories." They are, in chronological order, *Burr, Lincoln, 1876, Empire, Hollywood,* and *Washington, D.C.*

During the same period, Vidal invented a series of satiric comedies – *Myra Breckinridge, Myron, Kalki, Duluth.* "Vidal's development . . . along that line from *Myra Breckinridge* to *Duluth* is crowned with success," wrote Italo Calvino in *La Repubblica* (Rome). "I consider Vidal to be a master of that new form which is taking shape in world literature and which we may call the hyper-novel or the novel elevated to the square or to the cube." To this list Vidal added the highly praised – and controversial – *Live from Golgotha* in 1992.

Vidal has also published several volumes of essays. When the National Book Critics Circle presented him with an award (1982), the citation read: "The American tradition of independent and curious learning is kept alive in the wit and great expressiveness of Gore Vidal's criticism."

Vidal recently co-starred with Tim Robbins in the movie *Bob Roberts*.

BOOKS BY GORE VIDAL

NOVELS

Williwaw
In a Yellow Wood
The City and the Pillar
The Season of Comfort
Dark Green, Bright Red
The Judgment of Paris
Messiah
Julian
Washington, D.C.
Myra Breckinridge
Two Sisters
Burr
Myron
1876
Kalki
Creation
Duluth
Lincoln
Empire
Hollywood
Live from Golgotha

SHORT STORIES

A Thirsty Evil

————

PLAYS

An Evening with
Richard Nixon
Weekend
Romulus
The Best Man
Visit to a Small Planet

————

ESSAYS

Rocking the Boat
Reflections upon a Sinking Ship
Homage to Daniel Shays
Matters of Fact and Fiction
Pink Triangle and Yellow Star
and other essays
Armageddon?
At Home
Screening History
A View from the Diner's Club

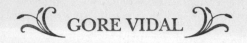

GORE VIDAL

A SEARCH
FOR THE KING

An *Abacus* Book

First published by EP Dutton & Co, Inc 1950
First published in Great Britain by William Heinemann 1979
This edition published by Abacus 1993

Copyright © Gore Vidal 1950

The moral right of the author has been asserted.

A CIP catalogue record for this book
is available from the British Library.

ISBN 0 349 10474 3

Typeset by M Rules
Printed and bound in Great Britain by
Clays Ltd, St Ives plc

Abacus
A Division of
Little, Brown and Company (UK) Limited
165 Great Dover Street
London SE1 4YA

For
DOT
and for
LOUISE NICHOLL

CONTENTS

INTRODUCTION

In the stacks of the library of the American Academy on Rome's Janiculum hill, I came face to face with M.I. Finley, whose *The World of Odysseus* had a great influence on me, not to mention on two generations of classical scholars. He was an American academic who had been driven out of his native land in the 50s when the spirit of Titus Oates was in the land. He settled in England; he became a leading authority on the Greek world of the Fifth Century BC. We praised one another politely. He had liked my *Julian* while I told him that, for *Creation*, I was mercilessly borrowing from him. I asked him about one of his colleagues who had written on Zoroaster. Was he reliable? "The best in the field." Finley's great dentures shifted slightly in his mouth. "Of course he makes most of it up, like the rest of us."

Now, as every dullard knows, the historical novel is neither history nor a novel. History means footnotes and careful citations from others tenured in the field, while the "serious" novel is about the daily lives of those who teach school and commit adultery; if they are *English* academics, they go to America or Zaire and experience a comical cultural shock. Curiously, imagination is not much admired in today's novels though demonstrations of literary theory through signs and signals are, if not very readable, highly teachable.

Until the last century the main line of imaginative literature had always been stories of the gods, heroes, kings of a people. From Aeschylus to Dante to Shakespeare to Tolstoi, what went on in the palaces or on Olympus provided the main line of narrative in verse, prose, drama. I think it a pity that, as a character in Saul Bellow's *Herzog* remarks, somewhere around 1840 the novel fell into the quotidian, to which Professor Herzog irritably asks, So where was it standing before it fell? The answer was in myth or history or whatever narrative is back of us.

Although I personally don't care for historical novels as such (I'm obliged to read history in order to write stories set in the past), I was drawn to write *A Search for the King* because it seemed to me a love story of great charm. My re-creation of Blondel and Richard Lion-Heart was deliberately more ballad than history. On the other hand, *Julian* took years to write and my description of how Christianity was, in a sense, invented at a series of fourth-century synods was based on a thorough study of the primary sources. Since I have never been an enthusiast of monotheism, the apostate emperor was the ideal protagonist. To my publisher's astonishment, the book was popular and continues to be read in most languages. Plainly, people find not only Julian but the times of interest. In due course, I received the least known literary award in the world, and the one most valued by me, the Greek Cultural Association's International Prize, awarded by "The Cities of Magna Graecia." Of course I live in Magna Graecia but even so.

With *Creation* I went back to Finley's period. One man, had he lived to be seventy-five, could have known Socrates, Zoroaster, the Buddha and Confucius. That anyone might have done so is highly unlikely – China was still very much off the as yet unbeaten Silk Road. But I created such a character, a Persian grandson of Zoroaster (whose dates are vague, to say the least). Cyrus Spitama is sent out on embassy by the Great King Darius and, later, by his heir Xerxes. If nothing else, this narrative is a sort of crash course in comparative religion and ethical systems; also, for the truly serious-minded, interest rates were running at a Thatcherite 20 per cent in the four societies – Greek, Persian,

Indian, Chinese – despite the absence of fax machines or, indeed, of any regular communication at all between the four.

The American publisher so disliked this book that it was sabotaged in-house; then, to everyone's amazement it became a bestseller. I am told that it is a cult book at Beijing though never translated because of the shifting party line on Confucius.

Why write historical fiction instead of history? Because, when dealing with periods so long ago, one is going to make a lot of it up anyway, as Finley blithely admitted. Also, without the historical imagination even conventional history is worthless. Finally, there is the excitement when a pattern starts to emerge. *Creation* is a favorite book of Noam Chomsky, whose studies in linguistics demonstrated that language is innate to the human brain and every child is born with an aptitude for learning language at a certain calculable rate. Chomsky noted my own astonished discovery that four separate literate societies, more or less at the same time, abandoned their ancient oral system of communication in favor of writing everything down.

From this one detail, I recognized – as did Chomsky – that it may well be that the human race has been programmed, like a human baby, and that the race goes from phase to phase, as one does from infancy to puberty to maturity and breeding to death. Chilling question: where are we now? Middle age or old age or – what? Is there a Lesson for Today in History? No. Today *is* history, too, and that's what makes it so interesting to examine.

Gore Vidal
Ravello, 1993

AUTHOR'S NOTE

In my grandfather's house in Washington there was an enormous attic lined with bookcases, containing several thousand volumes: constitutional history, law, currency reform, religion, copies of the *Congressional Record* (he was a Senator then) and, in the northeast corner, a hundred or so books which he allowed me to call my own. Most of my books were 19th century editions of fairy tales, a few books of history and a terrible (and forbidden) photographic history of the first world war. From the time I was five and could read until I was ten or eleven and moved away, I read everything I could and ruined my eyes and cluttered my memory with all sorts of ghosts whom I can no longer identify, characters and events which haunt me still with their insistent anonymity. But one story I've remembered clearly. I believe it was in the set called *The Book of Knowledge* and I reread it often, pondered it and, finally, in the fall of 1947 I decided to make a book of it.

The search of Blondel for King Richard was first invented in the 13th century *Chronicle of Rheims*. The facts, as facts often will, have nothing to do with this story. From all accounts Richard was captured by the Austrian Leopold, discovered by a duly constituted English committee, tried by a court and returned to his own country, having paid the first installment of a large ransom.

Blondel, an aging court poet, never figured in this somewhat involved political deal. But since seven centuries have chosen to believe a different story, I have sided with tradition and ignored the facts, for stories about friendships are not common: dark loving has always been the more popular theme. This, then, is a picaresque and a legend, one which has been repeated for centuries and one which has given me pleasure, in the memory of it and now in the telling of it.

New York City, September, 1949
G. V.

THE CAPTURE

Autumn: 1192

1

The sky was white now. At dawn the wind had begun to blow and, at dawn, three small ships landed at Zara. Wind cut the morning mist above the Adriatic, whitening the sky.

Blondel of Néel scratched himself and looked at the sea, shuddering as he thought of storms and ships foundering, of Palestine and, recently, Corfu. He yawned, stretched until his shoulders made a comfortable cracking noise: he thought how nice it would be to rest in some pleasant castle for a few weeks and exchange his Saracen lice for European ones. Perhaps he would write a ballad about the sea now that he was on land again: sea gods, storms, infidels, crusaders. He began to hum to himself as he walked up and down the quay.

The port of Zara was small, more oriental than European, with narrow crooked streets and brown-faced robed figures, chattering and doing business. Beyond the town he could make out low hills, wooded and dark. Between the town and the hills the land was cultivated but, for one accustomed to French fields, a little strange, wild even, and in places barren. The town itself was uninteresting. He liked cities and he liked countryside, but small ports, small towns and inconsequential castles bored him. Small towns were dangerous, too. It was better now, of course, than in the days before the first Crusade when strangers were apt to be stoned to death as a matter of policy. The armies had changed all that. People were now quite used to companies of men moving from west to east and, later, returning, scarred and seldom richer, from east to west.

Local sailors stood on the dock watching them; they made no move, however, to approach the edge of the dock where the three ships were being unloaded. Only two other ships, fishing vessels, were in the port.

The horses were being unloaded now. They were nervous: grooms soothed them, forced and coaxed them on to the dock. He saw his mare, already saddled, being led from the ship to the dock. She shied and he prayed his viol was uncrushed. It was his favorite instrument, brought all the way from France. He'd played this same viol the night Saint John of Acre fell.

A groom brought Blondel his horse; he mounted and rode to the other, crowded, end of the dock. Hooves made a deep hollow noise on wood as he rode through a crowd of men and horses. Baggage was being sorted and the King's lieutenants, Baudoin of Bethune and William of l'Etoug, were shouting orders. In the center of a confusion of grooms, knights and squires stood King Richard. He was frowning, talking quickly, and, to Blondel's surprise, he was wearing the long brown robes of a monk.

2

"Well, someone's got a horse, I see," said Richard irritably. "I think they've lost mine." He shouted for his horse, angry as he often was; Blondel, who had known him better these last three years than any man, found him, at times, frightening. He watched him as he smoothed his long, thick hair out of his eyes; at thirty-four Richard was graying and deep lines curved to the corners of his small mouth, half hidden by a short beard. He was a handsome man and vain; yet, though vain, he disliked ugly faces and he always had handsome people around him.

"Is this your disguise, sir?" asked Blondel.

Richard nodded, thoughtfully, watching the horses being unloaded. "I have to have some sort of disguise in Austria."

At Corfu Richard, hating the sea, had decided, quite suddenly, that the trip through the Mediterranean and up the coast of France would take too long and he had selected the overland route.

"But everyone will know you are in Austria with all this," said Blondel, looking at the crowd of knights and servants, baggage and horses.

Richard smiled. "I'll be a merchant returning from the East. We'll divide into two groups. The larger goes with the baggage and the smaller goes with me. Baudoin, William and you will be with me; we'll travel light . . ."

Baudoin of Bethune joined them: a young man with dark red hair who had been a friend of Richard's in the days when he was Duke of Aquitaine, before he was King. Baudoin had been at Chinon, Blondel remembered, when King Henry died and, as ex-favorite, he disliked Blondel and was as much disliked in turn, for Blondel, though he had spent most of his life among the nobles, still at times felt uneasy with them, secretly afraid of their hostility. Now, of course, he was a famous troubadour and Richard's favorite

3

and he was usually treated with respect, but there were a few, Baudoin among them, who disliked him and continually, through indirection, reminded him that he was only a peasant's son from Artois.

Baudoin announced that all the baggage had been unloaded, that the men were waiting for orders. The King looked about the dock, at the thirty or forty men who were to return with him: most of them, like himself, were Norman, not English, and Blondel watched him as he always did, fondly, anxiously: the way sailors take to watching the surface of the sea.

Richard was in a good humor. He turned to them and was about to speak when a man, dressed in unfamiliar livery, approached. He looked at the three, in doubt, obviously, whom to address. He spoke, finally, to Baudoin, the most richly dressed of the three. He spoke in Latin, bad Latin, thought Blondel, who had learned the universal language from a priest in Artois.

"I come from the Lord of Zara, who would know your identity and the reason for your visit here."

Baudoin started to speak but then, deciding not to, turned to the King, who said, in his most ingratiating, most political voice, "Tell the Lord of Zara that I am a merchant from Normandy and that I am returning from an, alas, unfortunate journey in the East. Some of these gentlemen who are now escorting me took part in the battle at Acre. They joined me at Corfu and for mutual protection we have decided to return together by land to Normandy. Kindly give our greetings to my Lord of Zara and entreat him to grant us leave to remain the night in his undoubtedly hospitable inns."

The man bowed and withdrew slowly, looking about him curiously. Then: "Come," said Richard. "They tell me there's an inn at the other end of the town, on the outskirts. We'll spend the day getting provisioned and tomorrow we'll leave."

It was good to be in the saddle again, thought Blondel: to be carried over the ground, rhythmically, naturally, not rocked helplessly about, the way the sea rocked one. He tapped his left saddlebag: the viol had not been broken. This made him happy and he began to hum one of his own songs.

He joined Richard, Baudoin and William. The four of them, accompanied by four mounted servants, left the others and trotted down the narrow dusty streets of the town. The natives stood back and watched them pass. Blondel noticed again how dark, how oriental they were. It would be strange, he knew, to be among the fair-haired people again. The Austrians to the north were lovely people, thought Blondel, who had always preferred day to night. He himself was light-complexioned though his hair was dark brown, almost as dark as Richard's.

They entered the square of the town, a small unprepossessing plaza with an old fountain, Roman in style. A new church dominated the square and Blondel, who preferred classic architecture, looked at this modern, Peak-windowed building with some distaste. Around the square were booths and carts: it was market day and the people milled about, shouting at one another, unaware of the strangers, intent on the business of living.

The King looked about him, glanced at the sun, determined his position and trotted through the crowd to the north side of the square, the others behind him. "I think we'll find the inn down this street," he said.

Two soldiers, in what Blondel supposed to be the service of the Lord of Zara, looked at them suspiciously, hearing

French spoken. They left the square hastily, riding at a fast trot down the dirty, urine-odored street.

In a few minutes Zara, a jumble of gray and pink buildings, was behind them, hiding the Adriatic. In front was open country, cultivated, spotted in plague fashion with the hovels of peasants. On a rise of ground a small and undistinguished castle stood, more wood than stone: doubtless the Lord of Zara's castle. They trotted across a narrow bridge which marked the end of the town. A shabby soldier, armed with a pike, let them pass.

Blondel breathed deeply. The air was clean here and he could smell the familiar odor of leaves moldering, of damp earth: he thought of Artois, of the villages in Picardy; it had been something like this in autumn, more beautiful, of course, though not so close to the sea. As a child he had loved the sea the way people who live not on it but near it love the sea: the sound of waves, the vision of vast distances and the sensation of violence observed on stormy days but not experienced, except romantically, beneath the curve of the watcher's skull.

"Here we are," said Richard, motioning to a large one-storied building made of wood and plaster and in need of repair. The innkeeper, a tall thin man with broken teeth, came out of the house, smiling and obviously frightened.

"We are merchants," said Richard grandly. "We have just arrived from the island of Corfu and we understand you give shelter to travelers."

The man blinked at them and then answered unsurely in Latin, "I give shelter for money."

"Good," said Richard dismounting. "You will take care of us tonight; our servants can sleep with the horses."

The man bowed, impressed no doubt by Richard's royal manner and the expensive dress of Baudoin. Both William and Blondel were simply dressed, while the King, in his monk's habit, succeeded in being the most conspicuous.

They went inside. Heavy, smoke-darkened beams held up a low ceiling. Several long tables and benches lined either end of the main room. Rushes carpeted the floor and dogs nosed about the room looking for discarded bones.

"Frightful," said Baudoin.

"Better than some castles," said Blondel, obscurely suggesting by his tone that Baudoin's own castle was like this.

"Depends, of course, where you visit," said Baudoin sourly.

Richard said, "You, Baudoin, and you, William, make arrangements with the innkeeper about supplies. We'll take as much as we can carry because, after tomorrow, we'll keep away from towns."

The two men left the room to find the innkeeper, and Richard turned to Blondel. "Now help me with a ballad. Something's gone wrong in the middle . . ."

They walked outside, composing Richard's ballad.

2

The fields stretched for miles before them; fields separated by woods and clustered about villages and occasional castles. This time of year the fields were dark, stubbled, the color of the earth, and the sun shone, when it shone, bright and hard. The air was clear and the wind blew sharply, cooled the days, created a singular clarity, knocked red leaves from the trees.

Autumn and the leaves fell: dry leaves covered the narrow country road, rutted with the deep marks of many carts; dusty roads, since the days were dry and clear. It was a time for making ballads, thought Blondel, and words came easily to him as they rode west, north-west towards Austria, the coast of Europe, and, finally, the King's island.

After two days of low country, of cultivated fields, they found themselves among hills, unwooded, covered with brush and vines and moss and, perhaps in another season, with flowers. Few people lived among these hills. They had been warned of bandits, but so far they had seen no one at all except shepherds, wild bearded men, shy and afraid of strangers.

One morning, the third day, they were able to look back from the summit of the first hill and see the land sloping, brown and fertile, into a vivid sea. A cluster of whitish buildings like discarded bones edged the sea: Zara.

Then they turned their backs on the sea and rode their horses down between hills into narrow valleys where, Blondel noticed, no birds sang: it was a strange bright country, to all appearances empty, existing in brightness and stillness. In the early mornings and late afternoons shadows fell across the valleys, the shadows of great rocks.

Trees grew in the valleys, most of them nearly bare, while their leaves, brown and rotting, covered the ground, rustled and whispered as the horses' hoofs brushed among them, hoofs that occasionally struck, with a ringing sound, leaf-hidden stones.

They followed a stream for several days. Willows grew on the banks and the clear water ran fast, swirling and bubbling over pebbles and the roots of trees, exposed by the water. They slept in the open each night and the sound of running water soothed them.

Richard and Blondel often sang together when they rode, side by side, at the head of the small company: followed by Baudoin and William; then the servants and baggage. Blondel, who had never known William well, grew to like him on this journey; he was in his early twenties, like most of the knights closest to the King, for Richard preferred the company of the young; older men were inclined to be not only cautious but, heresy, critical even of kings. William was dark-skinned with eyebrows which grew together in a straight line. He looked sullen but was not: he was pleasant, not too intelligent, pliable and, most important, completely dedicated to the King. Richard preferred him to the older Baudoin, who knew, Blondel suspected, too much about Richard's life before Chinon.

When Richard tired of singing they would ride silently between the trees, listening to the creaking of their saddles, to the murmur of the servants' voices behind them. Once, after a particularly long silence, as they rode over a barren hill, the King, reminded perhaps of death by the skull-like rocks that littered the top of the hill, talked of his brother John and the succession.

"*He* knows I've decided the succession." The way Richard said "he" Blondel knew that he was talking now of John. "He knows it goes to Arthur when I die. What's he doing, then? He's got no talent for politics, none at all; not much for intrigue either, though I could be wrong, and yet . . ." He stopped talking and squinted towards the west. There were more hills before them and, beyond these immediate hills, valleys, and, farther yet, the outline of far-off mountains. The King usually rechecked their position at night by the North Star; during the day, however, he calculated his directions from the sun and a somewhat inaccurate map that Blondel had found in Corfu.

They descended the hill to another wooded valley, a large valley shaped like a battered bowl.

"Well, they'll see what happens when I get back and John will find . . ." He stopped abruptly; Blondel knew that he seldom openly criticized his own family, since to criticize them would, in a way, be a criticism of himself, an admission of Plantagenet fallibility. He began again, speaking this time in a low voice, his eyes on the valley below them.

"I suppose the fault is Longchamp's. He's faithful and I can trust him, but that's all; it's a shame that the really capable men, the few one would like to trust, one can't."

"Do the English like him?" Blondel knew perfectly well what the English thought of Richard's chancellor.

"They dislike us all. But I think sometimes it would help if he'd learn just a little English, enough so he could read speeches anyway."

"I thought he knew English."

"No, he's never learned it and that's just the sort of thing which upsets the barons. But that's not so important. What he should have done was to have taken a decisive stand when John tried to separate the duchies. It would have been so easy to march down to Nottingham . . ."

They rode in silence. Richard didn't speak again for almost an hour; yet when he did he talked again of the succession. Ever since they had left England it had been on his mind. He talked of the succession a little wonderingly, as though it were some fascinating but abstract problem which he must, whether he liked it or not, consider.

They slept that night in the valley. At sundown Richard selected a camp site in a clearing at the foot of a small hill. Other travelers had been here recently, for there was a circle of flat stones in the middle of the clearing, enclosing ashes and the cold, blackened ends of logs. At the edge of the clearing, marked by ferns and long grass, was a spring. The servants made a fire, got water and prepared a meal.

Richard sat on a log near the fire and examined, dreamily, the hilt of his sword. Baudoin inspected the horses and

scolded the grooms in a low voice. They all spoke softly as
though in deference to the wilderness about them. Blondel,
having no duties, walked over to the foot of a hill and stood
beside a moss-streaked boulder and looked at the clearing
and thought of words. It was twilight now and Venus, a point
of silver, shone in the pale sky. The sun was gone behind the
hills, and in the east, above the tall forest trees, the sky had
turned slate. Quite alone, unaware of the others, he stood
and watched the darkness curve up the sky, rise out of the
forest and move darkly, star-dotted now, towards iron-
colored hills. The trees turned black, twisted skeletal shapes;
no wind stirred branches where a few dead leaves, brittle
and brown, broke with their irregular shapes the sharp outlines of the branches. The trees looked like the frozen figures
of a skeleton army, hostile, night-born and star-watched.

Then the sudden blaze of fire in the center of the clearing
transformed the sky, the forest and his mood. Red light
splattered the nearest trees and, as the fire grew large, shadows whirled on the edge of the forest. Now the sky was dark
by contrast and stars shone, cold and remote. The men gathered about the fire. One man, the cook, roasted game they
had killed that day and the others watched him. Blondel,
cheered somewhat by the sight of the fire (fire was home),
walked to the spring and washed the dust off his face and
out of his short blond beard. In Picardy the people had
been very clean, much cleaner than the English, for
instance; in Picardy they washed their bodies several times a
month and their faces even more often. His face clean, he
joined the King.

Richard sat by the fire at a distance from the others,
dreaming. Blondel sat beside him. Richard's face was tired
and his rather thin mouth drooped beneath the dark beard.
His eyes were half shut as he studied flames. He had taken

his boots off and his square, heavy-veined feet were pointed to the fire. Without turning his head he put his hand on Blondel's shoulder; he almost never looked people directly in the face because his close-set blue eyes made them nervous; cold and watchful eyes that appeared to see so much and actually, Blondel knew, saw very little, did not care to recognize another's reality or another's dream.

"We must pass through Austria?" asked Blondel at last; Richard's hand was heavy on his shoulder.

"Yes," said the King. He took the hand away, stretched, and then grasped his knees, resting his chin on his arms. "It would take too long to pass through Italy, too many mountains. No, we have to take the risk of crossing Austria. We'll be in Vienna soon."

"We're going to Vienna?" Blondel was surprised.

"Near Vienna anyway; we can't avoid it."

"It might be wise," said Blondel diffidently, "if we did."

Richard said nothing. With his big toe he sketched a map in the dirt: a dot for Zara, another for Goritz (the next town on their route), another for Barrin and, finally, a circle for Vienna. Then he sketched the Danube, mountains, all in considerable detail. His memory was excellent; he could remember maps, details of cities once visited, and, flatteringly, all of Blondel's ballads; he had a difficult time remembering names, however; he didn't remember people at all.

"And what about Montferrat's family?" added Blondel carefully; he was diffident but this must be discussed: they had not discussed Montferrat since Acre.

Richard shrugged. "We must take some chance. I suppose they still think I had him murdered but, since I've said I had nothing to do with it, that's that. I don't think they'd dare attack me. Leopold might but not these others; besides, it would mean a war and I don't think either Leopold or the Emperor wants a war now."

Yes, Richard was worried, thought Blondel. He had seldom heard him talk like this, minimize danger so casually.

"I wonder who *did* kill Montferrat," said Blondel suddenly, without thinking. He had never dared ask Richard this before because, actually, he had always suspected him of the murder. The Marquis of Montferrat had quarreled openly with Richard in Palestine, had sided with Leopold against him, and finally had intrigued, Richard claimed, against his life. During the height of Montferrat's quarrel with the King (a quarrel that had begun over certain spoils) he was assassinated. Everyone assumed that Richard was responsible and Leopold demanded that he be tried, an act of some courage since Richard headed the largest Christian army and was the victor of Acre as well. The King immediately denied all responsibility for the assassination, remarking, however, that it had occurred most opportunely and he, for one, would not mourn. Nothing was done in Palestine, though much vengeance was sworn as was the custom in such cases, since the family of Montferrat was large and influential. One of them, a man called Maynard, was Lord of Goritz: they were approaching Goritz now and the King had no army.

Richard looked at Blondel before he answered; eyes black in the darkness, glittering only when a flame, suddenly bright, threw light in his face, erasing shadows. "No," he said at last, "I don't know who killed him. Saracens possibly; perhaps his own men; perhaps Leopold: you know they were never really friends, those two. No, I don't know who killed Conrad. Eventually I might have but I didn't."

"What about Maynard of Goritz?"

"What about him? We'll be in Goritz only a few hours; there will be no reason for him to suspect I'm there and if

13

he does . . ." He played with his beard, forgot to finish his sentence; thought, no doubt, of danger.

The man who was cook announced that food was ready. Blondel, Baudoin, William and the King ate first; they talked very little and, when they did speak, their voices were low, depressed by the darkness and the forest about them. Then the men ate. When all the game was gone the men stretched out around the fire, prepared to sleep. Richard arranged a large fur-lined cape for himself on the ground; Blondel placed his own wool cloak near by. With his unsheathed sword beside him, Richard wrapped himself in the cape. "Sleep well," he said to Blondel and Blondel was aware he had smiled though his face was hidden.

"Good night . . ." He wrapped himself in his own cloak. The horses stirred uneasily and the men slept, all except the one who stood guard.

Blondel, on his back, faced the sky. The night was cloud-less and the black sky was full of stars. Like the smear of the wing of a luminous moth the Milky Way curved against blackness, surrounded by the other stars, arranged in regular patterns, dots of light which the ancients once thought were bits of fire.

A cool wind blew among the bare branches of the forest and the silence was disturbed by the creaking, the sighing of branches: a lonely sound.

He felt disembodied, unreal, as he watched the stars and thought of them. They were so remote, impersonal: the far-off lights of cities glimpsed at a distance in dreams but never approached or entered, not even in dreams. The night was vast; the sky was like half a globe placed over him and he was its center, the focal point of this half-globe. Stars existed outside himself and he beyond them; yet they were related to one another, mysteriously, surely: *he* was the center of vastness and aware. The specks of fire looked cold in the blackness and, thinking this, he was afraid, afraid of death, which would, in some way as yet unknown, rearrange this pattern, unite him, less his awareness, with these impersonal stars. He breathed deeply, and relaxed a little.

The air smelled of dead leaves, of damp, of wood smoke and of the undefinable smell of night. He glanced at the sleeping figure of Richard; his mouth was open and he was breathing heavily, like a child. Then Blondel slept, too, like a child.

They rode slowly over the hard, rutted road. The fields were deserted; peasants remained in their huts, warmed by small fires: thin lines of smoke rose in the sky over houses. More smoke hovered in a shifting mass over the town itself. Blondel rode beside Richard, while ahead of them rode Baudoin and William. The servants followed.

Blondel made conversation nervously. "You'll see the Queen again; it's been a long time, hasn't it?"

"Yes." Richard glanced over his shoulder as though afraid of being followed. "Yes, and she's not young any more."

Blondel smiled. "I meant your wife, the Queen."

"Oh, yes . . . Berengaria." Richard had married her the year before at Cyprus, before sailing for Palestine.

It had been a curious marriage, Blondel knew. Richard had been supposed to marry Alice, sister of Philip Augustus, the King of France, but Richard quarreled with him in Sicily. They had disagreed over Tancred, and Richard, anxious to be off to war, had seized Medina in Sicily for himself and Tancred, establishing the latter's right. Philip had naturally been indignant. Then Richard sailed for Cyprus and, needing revenue and provisions, conquered that island in his own name. While he was there word from his mother,

Queen Eleanor, arrived, reminding him sharply that he might not return from this crusade and that it was to the nation's interest he should leave an heir.

After examining the list (already familiar to him) of available princesses he selected Berengaria of Navarre and suggested to her father that a marriage be held immediately. Blondel remembered the day she arrived in Cyprus.

She was small, very young, and her eyes were large and dark. He even remembered how she was dressed: she had worn a small round veil on her head, held in place with a wreath of metal leaves. Her tunic was white, the color of virgins, and her cloak was deep red, the color of royalty. Richard received her casually but gracefully and allowed her one week to prepare for the wedding. The ceremony, when held, was simple. Baldwin of Canterbury officiated in a small chapel of the Cyprian fortress. Richard remained with her several days then, supposing (incorrectly as it later proved) that he had provided the throne with an heir, put her in another ship and, posterity arranged, sailed for the Holy Land. Later in the year she was sent home to Europe.

Blondel thought of this as they rode towards Goritz, talking of nothing, watching for danger.

The town was larger than Zara. A large monastery, Benedictine, Blondel guessed, dominated the outskirts of the town. The castle of the Count of Goritz was unimpressive and seemed in disrepair. The town itself looked old and much used, not by war or violence but by the slow debilitation of continuous living. The streets were not crowded and the few townspeople who saw them were neither curious nor hostile: many crusaders had come this way.

Houses were small, tile-roofed with small leather-hung windows which kept out cold and kept in smoke. They soon found a cookshop and here they stopped.

The air was hot and stifling inside; Blondel tried not to breathe too deeply, tried not to notice the heavy odor of smoke, burned meat and stale wine. Only a few travelers sat at the trestle tables. They stared at the newcomers.

A thick-set man in a stained tunic came forward and announced himself as master of the cookshop. Richard, through one of his own servants, an interpreter found in Corfu, ordered food for all of them. They seated themselves at an empty table: Richard with his back to the wall, Baudoin on his right and Blondel on his left.

"Like a tavern in hell," said Baudoin, coughing. The smoke grew thicker as their meal was prepared. Lumps of fat fell from spitted pigs into the fire and the logs hissed and smoked.

Richard, his eyes watering, nodded. "We won't stay long. When we finish send the servants to the market for food; we'll leave right away."

"We can't spend the night?" Baudoin was wistful in spite of the smoke.

"No, we have to avoid towns. Besides you always prefer open country, no smoke, clean air." Richard chuckled.

Food was brought and they ate greedily, tearing the meat apart with their hands, without knives. When they had eaten enough, when Blondel could hear his own stomach making digestive noises, Baudoin ordered the men to go to the market for supplies: it was then that they discovered none of them had any money. A chest of gold coins which Richard had ordered loaded at Zara was missing and was very likely with the other party. Blondel half-thought Richard might suggest seizing Goritz with his handful of men. He had seized Medina to help finance his crusade and he took Cyprus for the same reason. Money had never much concerned the King since it was so easily stolen. "We'll have to

17

sell like merchants after all," he said, finally, amused. He handed Baudoin a ruby ring which he usually wore on his forefinger. "Ask our host if he knows where this can be sold." Baudoin and the interpreter conferred with the master of the cookshop. Finally, after much discussion, Baudoin returned and said that a Jew attached to the Count's court would pay a good price for the ruby, providing it was real. Richard sent him off to the castle while Blondel took his viol and improvised a ballad as they waited.

He stopped, the *envoi* done, his own voice still in his ears; he was pleased with the words he had arranged, with the music he had made. He would write some of this down the first chance he got. He looked at the King for applause and the King smiled. "I like that: sad, but that's the way it is, always."

"Sing some more," said William, who was young and believed in ballads and loved women, sadness and battles.

Blondel sang another for the boy and the King hummed an accompaniment. They spent an hour singing and Blondel kept Richard from thinking too much of Maynard and Leopold and brother John. The master of the cookshop listened, too, with some pleasure.

The door of the inn opened and Baudoin, worried, entered, a tall thin man with him. Blondel went to the window and, drawing back the leather curtain, saw a dozen men-at-arms standing guard.

"Are you the merchant? the master of this group?" asked the tall man in good French, approaching Richard, who had risen and stood beside the table.

"Yes; my name is Villiers, a merchant from Normandy and at your service."

"Yes, yes." The tall man smiled, lines scarring his cheeks as he did. "I'm Maynard of Goritz, at *your* service, Master

Villiers. I was curious to meet you when my jeweler told me he'd been offered a valuable ruby for sale. I collect jewels, you know, and your ruby interests me. It's a fine stone, of course, but even more interesting, I think, is its historic importance. I'm well acquainted with all the crown jewels of Europe; not merely with the large pieces but even with such insignificant baubles as buckles and serving plate. I'm sure such things bore you since, obviously, you don't share my interest in historic jewels; if you did you'd never part with such a treasure. Henry, the late King of England, gave his wife, Eleanor of Aquitaine, seven ruby rings, one for each day of the week (not, I presume, one for each of the deadly sins). On the band of each ring he had engraved an 'H' and an 'E' entwined. This ring of yours is one of that set, Master Villiers, and I must say I'm curious to know where you found it." The Count stopped talking and looked at Richard.

Richard blinked and said, "I bought it in Cyprus." And Blondel shuddered, for the King lied badly.

"In Cyprus, Master Villiers? From the English King himself?"

"No . . . in the jewelers' market."

"Then I'm positive the ring must have been stolen from the King and I must send it to him in London. I'm told he is there now, or on his way. Perhaps he might even give me a reward, although," and Goritz chuckled, "we're sworn enemies. I belong to the Montferrat family, you know; distantly, I must admit, but blood is blood, I say, and murder is murder." The scars on either side of his mouth deepened.

"I . . ." Richard began and then he, too, chuckled.

"I understand," said the Count, "that the English King is still en route though, of course, he may already have returned. I'm told he was planning to pass overland to

19

Normandy but I'm sure he would never do that. Leopold sent me a message only the other day asking me if I had heard anything of him. I told him there were rumors, gossip, but nothing more."

"This is very interesting," said Richard evenly, "but, without sounding importunate, what price will you give me for this rare ring?"

"But, my dear Villiers, how can I give you anything for it when it belongs to neither of us? I must send it to England, of course."

"You . . ." Richard stepped forward suddenly and the Count of Goritz, no longer smiling, stepped back.

"My guards are outside," said the Count quietly. "You must leave Goritz immediately and be grateful I haven't seized you." The Count turned and left the room. Blondel watched him mount his horse.

Richard swore furiously, hit the table and kicked a stool across the room. The master of the cookshop, frightened now and awed by the recent appearance of his Count, ran from the room. Then Richard grew calm. He called the men about him. "Baudoin, William, Blondel and I will travel together. The rest of you must find your way back as best you can. Present yourselves to me in London when you arrive and I shall remember you. Now separate. In God's name."

They left the cookshop, leaving their account to be settled by the Lord of Goritz; they mounted, divided into two groups and left the town, galloping through the crooked streets of Goritz towards the cold, stubbled fields and windy forests to the west.

3

After a time the road became a narrow footpath which seemed about to disappear altogether in the tangle on the forest floor.

They rode in single file. The dark branches of tall trees locked over their heads. There was much underbrush, hiding rocks and rotting logs. Blondel had never seen such large trees: brown columns supporting the sky on a roof of twisted branches. A damp odor, of rot and mushrooms, of leaf mold and rain, hung in the air. Winter stood at the edge of the forest waiting and the birds had gone.

"You know," said William, who followed directly behind him, "what the cookshop man in Goritz said about this forest?" He spoke softly so that neither the forest nor the King could hear him.

Blondel shook his head and looked over his shoulder at him.

"He said it was haunted."

"I can believe that." Blondel smiled.

"According to him it was a great city once but a dragon came and changed the city into a forest."

Blondel nodded; he had heard such stories before. He never quite believed or disbelieved them. If he had the power and hated a city he would certainly change it into something: a forest was rather an obvious choice but no less effective. Such things seemed likely.

"The dragon," William continued, "still lives in the forest, and no one who knows this country ever goes through the center of the forest as we are doing. The dragon eats people." Young William seemed needlessly charmed by this idea, thought Blondel.

Richard, he knew, had been warned about the forest the

day before by a traveler; not so specifically, of course. Richard, however, had decided to take the risk, ignoring the danger from enchantments, aware of the advantages of crossing a haunted forest where local people would not dare follow.

At noon they stopped in a small clearing, a natural one, thought Blondel, examining it carefully. The ground was rocky and few plants grew beneath the trees which circled the clearing, their branches not quite meeting overhead: through the opening the sun shone brightly. As they had expected, there was a spring among the rocks, and water cold and clear as diamonds bubbled in it. They drank and then they ate some of the food they had stolen from one of the Count's farms on the edge of the forest.

"Odd place," said Richard, wiping water from his beard.

"They say the whole forest is enchanted, Sir. A dragon is supposed to live here," Blondel repeated and William nodded.

Richard smiled. "I hope they are wrong," he said. "I've enough trouble with Saracens and politicians; I've always left dragons to knights-errant and troubadours."

"Have you ever seen one?"

Richard shook his head. "No, but when I was a child there was supposed to be a dragon near Guyenne and every now and then, Midsummer's Day I think, they would lead a young man into the forest. No one ever saw the young man again or, for that matter, the dragon."

"I remember," said Blondel, "seeing some skulls of dragons in Artois. The Count of Blois, my old patron, had several bones of dragons. They were so old, though, they looked like stone."

For a time, forgetting politics, they talked of dragons and then they mounted again and rode out of the clearing.

The gloom of the forest was depressing for now no light shone through the close-knit branches overhead. There was no sound except that of their horses' hoofs, the tinkle of the bridles as they rode towards the center of the enchantment.

Then, from behind a group of great rocks, appeared the dragon's head: it was snakelike but as large as a horse's head, blue-green and glittering like metal. The eyes were small and unblinking. A snake's tongue darted out at them: rows of teeth, white and as sharply pointed as needles. Fascinated and horrified, unable to move, they watched the creature approach, slowly, from behind the rocks.

The neck was long and thin and the body heavy with a thick long tail, bescaled and gleaming as it moved, reflecting the dim light that penetrated the trees. Slowly the dragon moved towards them, its head swaying back and forth, branches and underbrush snapping as it moved. Richard shouted and the spell broke. Their horses shied and reared; then, at a gallop, Richard led them among the rocks, looking for some defense. Behind them they could hear the dragon approaching.

Richard ordered them to dismount. Their horses, thoroughly frightened now, were backed into a corner where they could not escape. Then Richard, sword in hand, led the three men between the rocks.

They faced the dragon.

The creature watched them, waiting, its head swaying. Finally, since they did not move, the dragon, opening and closing its jaws, approached. The next few minutes were so confused that Blondel never understood exactly what happened. Richard attacked the dragon and he had been beside Richard: the next thing he remembered was being thrown through the air and hitting the ground with a crash, losing his wind. For an instant he lay still on the stone-littered ground. He could no longer breathe and he twisted on the ground, strangling, trying to force air back in his lungs, gasping like a fish in the air. At last, with pain, he could breathe and he remembered the dragon. He scrambled to his feet and saw Baudoin nearby on the ground, groaning. Richard stood, his back against a rock, holding off the dragon. He couldn't move, Blondel saw; he could only keep the creature from striking. Frantically Blondel looked about for his own sword. He saw William standing on the other side of the creature, sword drawn, ready to strike.

Several feet away Blondel found his sword; clutching it, he rushed at the dragon. At the same time William attacked from the other side. The blade sank almost to the hilt in the dragon's flesh, glancing off a rib, probing near the heart. The creature twisted about, lashed with its heavy tail, striking William and throwing him into the air. Blondel leaped clear before the tail could strike and Richard plunged his own sword into the monster.

The neck writhed and the tail slashed back and forth in a semicircle. The tip struck Richard, knocking him down. The creature moved towards him, ready to crush. Shouting, Blondel threw himself against the dragon's side. Dark blood oozed from wounds in the green hide and the dragon, in pain, twisted about, ready to seize Blondel between sharp-toothed jaws.

But at that moment Baudoin and William attacked and, blood streaming down its sides, the dragon fled through the forest, crashing blindly into trees, smashing the underbrush with its great body.

Blondel helped Richard to his feet. The King was still a little dazed. His tunic was torn and his cloak was covered with dust and the blood of the dragon. All of them were streaked with dirt, their faces and bodies sweaty, covered with drying blood.

"So much for the dragon killing," said Richard weakly. And Blondel began to tremble with relief.

None of them was seriously hurt but all were bruised, scratched and dirty. Blondel's ribs ached when he breathed deeply; he hoped he'd broken nothing. "Let's find water," said Richard.

"Far from here," said Baudoin and they mounted again and rode into the forest.

Before nightfall they found a large spring, a pond in fact, with water smooth as a dark glass, reflecting the trees and fragments of the sky; a silent stream flowed out of the pond, between trees and stone-edged banks. They made a fire near by; then, their camp arranged, they took off their clothes and stepped into the cool water. The forest was quiet and as strange as ever. There was no wind and, though the winter had touched the air and waited upon the land, they were sheltered here, warm even, protected by the trees of this motionless forest, this transformed city, shadow-governed and dragon-guarded. The water was pleasantly cool, not cold the way it should have been on a winter's day. Perhaps, thought Blondel, it came from warm caverns below. He had seen such springs in Sicily. Some claimed there was fire deep in the earth: this water must rise from near the fire.

He shuddered as he stepped into the water, not from cold but from relief. Carefully he slipped into the water. Smooth, slimy rocks covered the floor of the pond and, underwater, he stepped carefully from rock to rock: like running in a dream. William stood on the bank, slim and boylike. Baudoin swam easily about the pond while Richard stood waist-deep in the water and splashed his face and chest: thick-set, with heavy muscles across his shoulders and short strong muscles in his arms; on his chest copper-colored hair grew in the shape of a cross.

Blondel looked at his own body, floating on the surface of the black water. He was strong though not so strong as the King. His muscles were longer and the hair grew down his chest in a narrow line. His legs were longer than the King's; he flexed them, made the muscles ripple underwater: this hurt him, though, made him ache and he relaxed, allowed the water to support him.

The four men like four pale ghosts swam in the black water. Was Lethe like this? he wondered. There were no problems now; almost no memory. He glanced at Richard, who was swimming noiselessly across the pond, unworried by the usual thoughts of kings. Four white figures, without memories, without histories, moving in black water within an enchanted forest where no birds sang, no creatures moved except themselves and the figures of magic. This was better than life, akin, perhaps, to death. Four ghosts, pale as ice, silent as air, drifting in a place of magic.

4

Shortly after noon the next day they reached the end of the forest and found themselves in open country, partly cultivated; a well-defined road, Roman doubtless, ran in a straight line over the fields and between smooth hills.

Baudoin sighed and turned to Blondel, almost cordially, and said, "Thank heaven we're out of that."

Blondel wanted to say something: it was always difficult to answer a suddenly cordial remark from someone disliked; fortunately, however, William commented.

"At least we killed a dragon," he said grinning.

"I'm not so sure he died," said Blondel. "He's supposed to be magic after all."

"Nonsense," said Baudoin. "It was just an animal like any other. People I've known who've been in Africa have seen a lot stranger-looking animals; much larger, too."

"Maybe," said William, unconvinced. "Still ours was a real dragon. Old men say that once there were millions of them in Europe but the people killed all except a few."

"I've seen their bones in Sicily," said Blondel. He spurred his horse and joined the King who rode a few yards ahead of them.

"If only there were more trees," Richard murmured as they rode.

They were plainly visible for miles around. Blondel looked about the countryside for signs of life. In the distance he could see, at irregular intervals, the huts of peasants and far away in the east, on a hill no different from the surrounding hills, he made out the shape of a castle, turreted, set like a crown on the hill. "Look!" he exclaimed, pointing it out to the King.

Richard nodded. "I know about that place: belongs to a wealthy knight, a relative of Leopold's; all this is his land ... if only there was more cover."

They had ridden a few miles farther, the winter sun slanting obliquely in their faces, when William started and called out. They turned and saw a group of armed men, dressed as crusaders, riding towards them at a gallop. Unable to escape, they reined in their horses and waited. The men surrounded them.

"Surrender, Richard!" shouted the leader in French.

Richard drew his own sword and the others drew theirs. He glanced about him, judging his position. Then he roared a command and charged the leader of the group. Blondel followed, close behind. With a clanging of metal they broke the circle, the leader of the would-be captors fell and

Richard, still followed by Blondel, galloped towards the hills. William followed him. He looked back only once and saw William behind him; Baudoin was fighting with the Austrian soldiers near the road.

Wind in his face, his legs wet with horse's sweat and his mouth dry with fear, he rode behind the King, rode among the hills until, at last, they felt they were safe, hidden from the soldiers; just as they were about to stop, finally, in a dried-up, rock-littered river bed, Richard's horse stumbled and threw him on the rocks.

Blondel and William helped the King to his feet. His hand was bleeding and he swore furiously. Then they looked at the horse and saw that one of its forelegs was broken; William, the bravest, killed the animal and Richard mounted behind Blondel. "We'll have to take our chances at the castle." Blondel did not argue; he knew now that none of them would ever reach England.

It was just past sundown when they arrived at the castle's gate. They hadn't spoken since the fight with the Duke's men: they took it for granted that the attackers were Austrian. No one had mentioned Baudoin either and Blondel wondered if he'd been killed or only captured. Richard said nothing, frowned and was, Blondel could see, frightened.

The gate of the castle had not yet been closed; it stood half open in the stone wall; the keep was made of wood, new-built and in the Norman style.

"State your business." A man-at-arms stood before them, the gate's guard.

"Crusaders," said Richard, "returning to our native France. I lost my horse on the road, an accident. As fellow knights and Christians we would present ourselves to the lord of this castle."

The man held a torch up to their faces. They looked, Blondel knew, like thieves with their dusty faces and torn cloaks but they wore the mail of knights; Richard had long since thrown away the monk's habit.

"Enter," said the man, uncertainly. "The lord of the castle, Sir Eric, is just returned from Palestine himself; they are preparing his sister's marriage to a countryman of yours."

"And who's that?" asked Richard politely.

"Sir Roger of Aubenton, he . . ."

"Aubenton!" Richard almost shouted with delight. Then: "Sir Roger is an old comrade of mine. Where can I find him? is he here now?"

The man was impressed and, no doubt, relieved. "I'll send a guard to take you to him." He called one of several men who were playing dice by the gate. "Take this knight . . . what's your name?"

"Richard . . . of Guyenne," said the King, using his old title.

"Take Sir Richard to Sir Roger's apartments. And if you see the Austrian captain on the way tell him his horse is ready."

Blondel began to pray silently, automatically, invoking all the gods and saints.

The courtyard was full of men and their horses. Pages with torches darted, like giant fireflies, back and forth with messages, doing errands. Light streamed from the narrow windows and, for a moment, Blondel was weak and hoped they would be captured so that they could be with people again, move in rooms, in light and warmth. They dismounted and the guard led them into the castle.

They crossed the great hall where servants were preparing dinner and dogs sat on the rushes watching spits turning over the fire. In a small room off the hall they found Sir

Roger; he was pulling a tunic over his head.

"Sir Richard of Guyenne," announced the guard.

"Who? Richard of . . . Good Lord!" He pulled the tunic down over his head. "Leave us, guard." When the man was gone he embraced Richard. Then he stood back and looked at him with amazement. At last he laughed and said, "I see now why people have taken to calling you Lion-Heart. You walk right into the castle of Leopold's cousin on the same day a party of soldiers has been sent out to capture you . . . you know, some would say Your Majesty was mad."

Richard sat down wearily on a bench, resting his bandaged hand on his knee (a piece of Blondel's cloak had provided the bandage).

"No, not mad; I know all that. The Duke's men attacked us a few hours ago. They captured or killed Baudoin of Bethune but we escaped. Then my horse broke a leg. This seemed our only chance to find a horse; as for the risk . . ." he shrugged.

Sir Roger nodded; he was a pale man with yellow hair. "They only captured Baudoin and, I suppose, they'll hold him for ransom. He's in no particular danger. I'm surprised the man at the gate didn't suspect anything."

Richard smiled weakly. "I don't think it would occur to him that a hunted man would join the hunters. What sort of man is Sir Eric?"

"Good enough, I suppose . . . the Duke's protégé and very ambitious. You can't stay here, you know."

"No," said Richard, "we can't. Can you get me a horse and provisions? I don't plan to walk to Normandy."

Sir Roger nodded. "Wait for me here," he said and he left them. Blondel and William sat beside Richard on the bench.

"Can you trust him, Sir?" asked William.

"I have to," said Richard and they waited. Blondel's mouth

filled with saliva as he smelt the odor of roasting from the great hall. The noise of voices, men and women mixed, grew louder as they assembled in the hall; someone played a viol and began to sing (not very well) and Blondel wanted desperately to be with them, to be warm, to be surrounded by people again, to have an audience: but they must ride tonight over frozen fields and sleep in the open on hard ground.

Sir Roger reappeared. "I've a horse for you, Sir," he said quickly. "Saddlebags are filled; you must go right now, though. The captain of the guard told the Austrians something and they're curious to see you; suspicious, too, I think."

Richard stood up. "Thank you, Roger." He shook the knight's hand. "See that Baudoin is not harmed."

"I will."

"If you come to England you'll be rewarded."

"Thank you, Sir."

They crossed the great hall, unnoticed in the crowd. Sir Roger escorted them to the gate and told the captain of the guard that Sir Richard was carrying messages to the Duke in Vienna and would not spend the night.

They waved at Sir Roger, who stood in the gate, the light of a torch behind him; he waved back. Then they broke into a slow trot and rode down the hill towards the empty fields. Overhead a new and fog-wrapped moon shone grayly upon their path.

5

For half that night they rode. The moon shed a dull light on trees and hills. While peasants slept in their dark huts they rode and, finally, at the moment when men in castles, tired of lovemaking, were ready for sleep, they made a camp in a river bed, fixed a small fire and slept.

White frost like a pattern of lace covered the ground. The sky half gray, half dark, the sun still behind the horizon, day barely begun, they awoke and rode northward.

Blondel shivered in the cold, ached from his bruises. His cold hands were red as raw meat and he wondered if they might not freeze, gripping the reins forever. A sharp wind blew, piercing his ears, numbing the brain: his eardrums ached. He looked at Richard and saw he was oblivious to the cold, as kings should be. But William, who was only a knight, and a boy-knight at that, suffered, too. He kept his lips tight shut, however, and imitated the King. Blondel envied him because he believed so many things which an older man could not believe: that kings felt no discomfort if they were brave, that Saracens were evil and Christians good, that the crusades were begun to free the tomb of Christ. Blondel smiled grimly at the wind as it stung his lips. There was treasure in the East and trade routes to India and the silk countries. Every country in Europe wanted control of the East and, happily, someone had remembered that Jerusalem contained the tomb of Christ and so the kings gathered armies, received Papal blessings and, accompanied by mitred bishops, sailed for Palestine and there fought the brown people, sure of the righteousness of their cause and well aware that the death of heathens was nothing compared with the freeing of a dead God's tomb.

Richard, at least, was no hypocrite in private and Blondel was glad of that. The King always spoke in terms of loot, trade routes and strategic positions. The only time he ever mentioned the Sepulchre was in speeches made for the benefit of churchmen and of other princes who, in turn, made similar speeches for his benefit.

It was also a good idea, Blondel knew, for the knights to have a place to go, a place where young men could fight and kill without fear of reproach, where they could be brave and well rewarded, where they could live with one another, do violence together, free from the restraining influence of women and a comparatively secure society. Seen thus, Blondel decided, the crusades were useful and such good things outweighed the discomfort, the pain, the last sharp arrow or curved sword which so often, bloodily, ended the life of a youth born more than a thousand miles away in a gentler place where hills were green, not brown, not shaped of dust. In a sense the death of young men in battle was beautiful: they would not grow old now, or ugly, or die of some slow and shattering disease. They would have the good fortune to die in sudden violence, still vigorous and strong, their blood giving a brief brilliance to the brown sad land of Palestine. Yes, it was better that they be united here and kill the Saracen than remain at home in Europe and, for want of other diversion, kill one another there. He and Richard would discuss all this one day when they could sit peacefully before a fire and reminisce, an old king and an old troubadour . . . if either lived to be old. Richard, he felt, would say much the same things: young men must fight . . . yes, it was good, poignant, of course, yet beautiful, containing, as all great beauty must, the tragic proportion. His own ballads were sad even when he spoke of love, as he almost always did. But though he sang of love he knew that love was so much more than what a man felt for a woman, a man begging a woman to receive him: the conventional structure of a ballad, plea to the Lady. For the Lady was many things: all love, all great emotion, battles. The Lady was the comradeship of knights. The Lady was beauty. The Lady was the mother of God. So she stood as a symbol for many things, for all the passion and all the beauty in the world. He had discovered her when he was sixteen, walking in the warm summer-green fields of Artois, walking, for the first time, with someone else, with a young girl: the Lady.

All of his ballads were written to the Lady.

Now the sun rose behind them, bright and chilly. He felt light, only faintly warm, strike the back of his neck and he imagined he was warmer, that the light warmed him. He thought of fireplaces with huge crackling logs and yellow flames; he thought of summer in the fields of Artois; he thought of making love.

They paused for food at noon, made a fire so small that it only made the cold worse by contrast. Then the nightmare ride continued. The trees, like the skeletons of every Saracen ever slaughtered, passed them in mocking parade. Hills like the skulls of dead soldiers watched them. Open country, frost-marked and furrowed, the face of a dead giant looking skyward, stretched before them to the edge of the sky. At times it seemed as if they themselves barely moved, that the trees, the hills, the scarred earth were moving, rushing towards some distant abyss, some final grave beyond the earth, passing the travelers by, deserting them to emptiness and to the embrace of cold. The sun rose, curved and fell from the east to west; then rose once more to fall again from the top of the sky to the western mountains. Small fire succeeded small fire at various intervals, like vivid roses dropped on snow.

The cold was always present; it rode beside them, their fourth companion. At night it hovered outside the small radius of the fire and when they rode again it rode beside them, mounted on wind.

The King fell ill. One morning he woke, coughing and breathing hard. When Blondel suggested they build up the fire and spend the day, or at least an hour or two, there, Richard grew furious and, unsteady, mounted his horse and rode north. They followed.

But fortunately that evening they came to a broad river and beside the river was a small town which was called, according to a villager, Oberhass, or some such name for none of them spoke German and the villager knew no other language. As they rode down the streets Blondel thought he had never seen such a wonderful town.

The buildings were of timber, solidly built and not very high. The roofs were steep and covered with tile. Most of the windows were sheltered against the cold and the central street of the town was newly cobbled: the town seemed prosperous, a new town. The square was ordinary with the usual fountain: this time an ornately classical one decorated with dolphins spouting water which, when it hit the basin, froze.

An Italianate church dominated the square. On two sides of the square were the houses of the rich; on the fourth side, opposite the church, was an arcade: the market. Everything was deserted today, however. They paused in front of the church and, as they paused, a priest came out of one of the side doors.

Blondel addressed him in his best Latin: "Tell me, Father, where we might find lodging for the night." The priest told them of a house where travelers were welcome; they thanked him and soon found this house.

At first Blondel thought he might faint in the heat of the room. Gusts of heat scorched his face, making his ears ring and burn. The King staggered to a bench, sat down, resting his face in his hands, unable to move. William stood dumbly, looking at the fire. Finally it was Blondel who made arrangements with the master of the house. He told him they would rest here several days; he looked at Richard, half-expecting protest but none came. They were French knights returning to their own country. They had fought with bandits on the way; their baggage had been seized and their attendants killed. He made a convincing story; he spoke in Latin which the master of the inn understood imperfectly but, being a man of pretensions, pretended to understand, nodding often with an air of spurious intelligence.

They helped Richard to bed; he was given the best bed: in fact, the only bed in the inn. Blondel helped him out of his mail, placing his sword beside him; the King was unconscious by the time he had placed a blanket over him.

Then Blondel and William sat before the fire and drank wine, warming their hands. Blondel wondered if he could ever burn the chill out of his bones. At least his blood was circulating again, pounding in his ears, flushing his face and temples as though it might burst through the skin.

William, beside him, held his hands in front of the fire, ready to plunge them Scaevola-like into the flames. "At last," William sighed.

"At last," said Blondel, and he hoped they would never leave this house, this room, this fire.

Richard was delirious that night. Blondel stayed up with him, wrapping him in blankets and cloaks which were soon thrown to the floor; he gave him water from time to time. In the other room William slept like a puppy, curled among the rushes before the fire.

Light was already coming through the windows when Richard began to sweat and the coughing stopped; he slept.

Someone shook Blondel. He rolled over on his side. For a moment he was frightened. Then he saw William was shaking him. "Wake up; it's after noon."

Blondel stretched on the floor. "How is he?" he asked at last.

"Better, I think. He's not out of his head now but he's very weak."

"Coughing stopped?"

"Almost."

Richard lay on his back, looking at the ceiling beams. His face was yellow-white and, for the first time, Blondel was aware that he was not a young man any longer, that his face was lined and, relaxed, tired and bitter. He didn't look like the Lion-Heart now.

"Sir," he said in a soft voice.

The head turned: red veins showed in the whites of his eyes. The lips tried to resume their usual expression of command but the effort was too great. "I didn't sleep well," he said at last, weakly, petulantly.

"I knew; I was with you."

"It was you then? Good. I thought . . . I thought I was some place else."

It was several days before the King could walk and when he did it was like a child, unsurely, his legs strange to him.

When he was well enough, days later, they sat by the fire together and talked, made plans for the journey across Austria and France. They were, they discovered from the master of the inn, only a few miles from Vienna. As soon as the King could ride they would leave. Now they would sit and warm themselves and talk.

Blondel recalled one evening when the armies of the allies were quartered at Ascalon a few miles from Jerusalem; a year ago this month they had been there. There had been a meeting in Richard's tent. He had sat on a chair which had once belonged to a Saracen prince; a chair set with jewels and inlaid with gold. He was triumphant then: red-faced from the sun and wind, vigorous, sure of victory, already the master of Acre and first of the Christian princes here. He sat with Guy of Lusignan and Conrad of Montferrat and they argued over who should govern Jerusalem. They had argued over the division of spoils and Richard had insisted blandly that he divide the treasure for them and they resented this bitterly; they were helpless to oppose him, however.

Blondel remembered that evening vividly. It had been the great moment of Richard's career in Palestine. He had taken Acre and now, presently, he would take Jerusalem and drive Saladin into the desert. Victory had made him arrogant, Jovian in his humor: no one dared contradict him. Once he had thrown a baron to the ground for suggesting an alternative attack to the one he himself had decided upon. He treated everyone casually, with superior and mocking indifference; everyone except Blondel, whom he consistently treated gently, his troubadour and his friend.

Conrad sat at a table in the tent that night, drinking Italian wine as they talked of spoils. Guy of Lusignan, a quiet man, florid and stout, listened, spoke seldom. Blondel himself sat in a corner of the tent, his viol on his lap, waiting for the meeting to end when he would play for the King. They talked for hours and then they quarreled; Conrad threatened to withdraw his troops and Richard laughed and said that he hoped the Lord of Montferrat would, by all means, withdraw his troops, thus simplifying the problem of the spoils. Conrad stormed out of the tent and Guy of Lusignan followed him. Richard laughed, ordered wine, and Blondel played for him. Soon after this Conrad was murdered and, shortly after that, Richard's attack on Jerusalem failed.

Richard talked about this before the fire. If he *had* taken Jerusalem . . . ah, how different things would have been. He would have been greater than the Holy Roman Emperor; instead, however, he had been forced to make a three years' truce with Saladin and then, because of the trouble between John and Longchamp in England, he had no opportunity to break that truce, to seize Jerusalem, for he was forced to return home.

Casually, Blondel mentioned the Saracen prisoners and Richard frowned and Blondel was furious with himself for having mentioned them. Richard's army had taken almost three thousand prisoners; then, to the shock of the other Christian princes who were not easily shocked, Richard had had all the prisoners killed.

"It was necessary," he said, scowling into the fire, studying patterns of yellow-red flames. "We couldn't support that many prisoners and, certainly, we couldn't free them. There was nothing else I could do; besides, the Church condoned it: they were only heathens." But Blondel saw that it troubled him and he wondered why, since Richard was a soldier and used to the unpleasant expedience of war; perhaps there *was* an instinct in men to preserve life which, if not as strong as the instinct to kill, was, at least, always present as a balance to destruction: a need to affirm, by such objective action as an act of mercy, the importance of personal gesture before the general and the inevitable death of knowledge.

In recognition: "They killed our men; *they* never took prisoners. I did what they did. I did what every general from Alexander to me, sooner or later, has been forced to do. And then what does the month, the hour of a man's death have to do with it? or the manner of his dying? *Sub specie aeternitatis* . . ." he quoted suddenly and paused, unsure; wondering if he had proved something, if he'd stated an original idea with a bit of Latin. Then: "Yes, none of it will matter then. In a hundred years Normans, Saracens, Plantagenets will all be dead and different generals will fight new wars in different lands and we'll be so much dirt within stone tombs or scattered on the hills of Palestine. *Then* who will care if Richard killed three thousand Saracen prisoners? and if they care how can it touch us? On a Tuesday they were killed; some would have died in battle within the week, more within the month, even more within the year and, in fifty years, most would be dead of disease. Perhaps it was my function to make a common day for their dying. I was the instrument of a swift death. God made me for a king, and fate, which is God-controlled, sent me to that country: their death, then, was no more my doing than my birth was theirs." He paused and then he turned to Blondel and said, "Do you ever think of dying?"

"Yes . . ."

"No, I mean of course you do but do you ever *think* it, consider it, examine the thought till your head spins?"

Blondel nodded, understanding this, surprised that Richard had ever had such thoughts. "Yes, I've thought of it, realized there was no avoiding it."

Then Richard growled, "Sickness is making me a philosopher; better to fight with no thinking and kill three thousand men if necessary: anything's better than this thinking." He slapped his leg. "This flesh will fall from the bone soon enough without my thinking of it."

They talked then of troubadours.

Each day Richard grew stronger; soon he would be able to ride again. The master of the inn, a congenial man, had received without comment Blondel's instructions not to mention their presence; he gave what he thought were convincing reasons and they felt as safe as it was possible to feel so close to Vienna.

One afternoon while William slept and Richard was helping the servants fix a broken spit Blondel went walking in the town.

He visited the church and disliked it: too much light and color. Everything was brighter than the English and Norman churches. He preferred the secrecy, the promise of magic in the dark and cavernous churches of his own country. As he stood in the doorway, a priest, the same he had spoken to the first day, came up to him and inquired about his friends.

Blondel told him one had been ill.

The priest nodded sympathetically, "A familiar illness in this country. Often people die of the fever and coughing. You're from France, aren't you?"

Blondel said yes. "I'm from Artois and my friends are from Paris. We were in the service of Philip Augustus."

"A noble Christian king," said the priest piously. He was a plump little man with round soft hands, pink and dimpled. "And you have, of course, been fighting the Infidel. Oh, how I envy you! Many's the time I've asked my bishop to let me go out there, to do what little I can for our Cause but, alas, I'm needed here, too. Each must serve in his designated way." The priest glanced tenderly at his own hands, as though admiring their softness.

Blondel excused himself; he had heard this particular complaint before and not always from priests.

He strolled across the square. The sky was pale, colorless, and there was little wind to stir up the cold in the air. A few people were selling and buying within the arcade. He stopped beside the fountain and watched the women cracking with stones the surface of the ice and drawing water. The dolphins trickled water through ice-choked mouths.

He was watching the women when, suddenly, he was aware that someone was standing behind him. He turned slowly; he would not show surprise. Seven armed men stood behind him. They had been in the square for some time: he'd heard no sound of horses. One of them approached him and

41

inquired, in French, where he was going.

He gave a false name and said he was returning to Artois. Over the man's shoulder he saw the pale round face of the priest watching him.

The officer asked more questions: how long had he been here? with whom? why had they stayed so long in this town? He answered all these questions calmly; he surprised himself with his own coolness. Of course, he had been preparing for this for days. The only thing that disturbed him was the crowd of women staring at him and the righteous expression on the face of the priest. Then the officer asked him, politely, if the man who'd been ill was, by any chance, Richard, the English King.

"Of course not." He even managed to laugh. "We are French knights."

"But I have reason to believe that your companion is Richard. It would save everyone much trouble if you would admit this now."

"Ask him yourself," said Blondel and he started to walk away. The officer stopped him. "We prefer to ask you," he said. Then Blondel understood. They didn't dare force an admission from Richard; the Duke had probably forbidden them to touch him. The only alternative was to get either William or himself to confess.

"I suggest we go into the church," said the officer and Blondel was led to the church; bowing slightly, the priest received them and led them down a narrow staircase into a damp and icy crypt. He lighted a torch for them and then, with another bow, excused himself. Without a word, one of the men removed Blondel's cloak and tunic and another tied his hands to a ring in the wall. The skin of his breasts contracted in the cold air. One of the men handed the officer a whip and Blondel wondered, idiotically, where they had managed to find a whip so quickly. Had they had it with them all the time? or had the priest produced it? "Is your companion King Richard?" asked the officer in a gentle voice.

"No," said Blondel and he waited a long time for the whip to fall and, after a time, he heard it whining in the air; then, with a crashing sound, it fell across his back. His legs gave way and he hung by his bound hands. Then it fell again; too quickly this time: bright stars of pain flashed behind his eyes. He kept his eyes tight shut, to shut out the pain if that was possible, to make the pain more like a dream, less real. Now the whip seemed to pound his back regularly, to cut so hard that the center of his back became numb and only where the end of the whip, like a tongue, curled, could he feel the burning unbearable pain. After a time his body collapsed and he hung limply, barely clinging to the slippery edge of consciousness. What had been constellations of brilliant stars now became bands of blurred light. And somewhere, beyond the light, a voice kept repeating, "Is this man the King?"

Finally, just to stop the whining sound of the whip in the air he whispered, "Yes, he's the King." For a while there was nothing. Then he was conscious of being handled by men. He opened his eyes and saw that he was being lifted off a horse. They were in front of the inn; since he couldn't walk they dragged him inside and dropped him on the floor where he lay motionless, glad to be let alone. The tunic had begun to stick to his back as the blood dried; it hurt him to move but he knew he must: he pulled himself up on one elbow.

Richard, unarmed and surprised, stood on the hearth with a frightened servant: they had been fixing the spit.

"This man tells us you're King Richard," said the officer.

Blondel tried to get up, to say something, anything to explain but Richard, seeing blood on the back of his tunic, said, in English, "I understand." Then he turned to the officer and said coldly, in the harsh voice which always frightened men, "How could you touch my troubadour? How could you? Answer me!"

"It . . . it was necessary, Sir," said the officer, reacting as all men did to Richard's anger. "He wouldn't admit you were here."

"And why should he? Why should it be any concern of yours that I'm traveling through Austria? By whose order are you here?"

"By the Duke Leopold's, Sir."

"And what are your instructions?"

"To arrest you, Sir, and take you to Vienna."

There was silence. Richard stared at the officer until that unhappy man looked away; then he said quietly, "I refuse to be arrested. Neither you nor Leopold nor the Emperor has the right to arrest me."

"Then . . . we must take you anyway, Sir."

Richard grabbed the spit, a pointed and dangerous bit of metal, as effective as a sword. "Try," he said and he shouted for William over his shoulder and the boy, sword drawn, joined him on the hearth.

"You're making this very difficult for us, Sir," said the officer.

"I mean to," said Richard agreeably. "William and I will kill a number of you before I'm seized. I wonder which ones we'll kill . . ."

"But you're in Austria, Sir; outnumbered by a whole country. It would be very easy to kill you."

"Oh, not easy at all," said Richard. "If I were a guest in a castle, yes; it would be easy since I could be poisoned and the world would learn I died of illness, but here, in a small town with many witnesses, it wouldn't be at all simple. You're an educated man. You know what the word 'regicide' means . . . and the penalty."

"I do."

"All Austria could be excommunicated for my death, not to mention a war with England."

"I know all this, Sir. The Duke instructed me to take you alive."

"Very sensible of him. My ransom will get him out of debt. However, I refuse to surrender myself to you. Go and tell Leopold to come in person and perhaps he can persuade me to surrender. Actually, I can only surrender, properly speaking, to an emperor but, unfortunately, the nearest Emperor is at Frankfort; so bring me a Duke." Richard grinned at them and flourished the spit.

The officer, unable to handle this situation, shrugged finally and said, "The inn will be surrounded until I get instructions from Vienna so don't try to escape. Good day, Sir." The officer saluted and withdrew.

Richard and William carried Blondel into the bedroom. William brought water and strips of cloth the innkeeper had given him; gently, Richard washed his back. "I'll see to those men," he said grimly. "I'll see to the whole lot, including Leopold. I never thought he would dare do this to me, and he wouldn't on his own. The Emperor consented, and that means . . . how do you feel ?"

"Better." Blondel buried his face in the blanket. "I'm sorry," he said; he wanted to cry like a child, and Richard, like a father, said, "That's all right. You should have told them when they first asked you. It would have made no difference: they were bound to find me sooner or later." He fixed the bandages with extraordinary gentleness, made him

45

drink some wine and then told him to sleep and he slept. Voices awakened him.

His entire body was sore, every joint ached when he moved and his lips were dry, hot with fever. From the next room he heard men talking. Carefully, painfully, he got out of the bed and crawled (he could barely stand) to the door of his room; rough cloth hung in the doorway. He pushed back a corner of it and he saw Richard and William again on the hearthstone, swords drawn. The innkeeper moved about unhappily and, outside, Blondel could hear the noise of horses and many men.

There was a knock on the front door and the innkeeper, first clasping his hands beneath his beard, no doubt in prayer, opened the door. A tall fair man, still young, wearing a dark cloak and a crimson tunic, entered the room, followed by attendants and guards. Blondel recognized him immediately: it was Leopold, a weak-faced, rather handsome man with a small chin. He smiled pleasantly when he saw Richard, bowed ceremoniously and greeted him in exquisite Latin, enumerating his titles with reverence and accuracy.

Richard returned his greeting with the same ceremony.

"I was very disturbed, Your Majesty," said the Duke easily, "that you refused my invitation to join me in Vienna. I understand that my invitation was clumsily put and for that I apologize. Several weeks ago I heard you were in my country, but not until a few days ago did I hear exactly where you were staying. Have you quite recovered from your illness?"

"I have."

"I'm glad. It would give me much pleasure if you would be my guest in Vienna. We haven't seen much of one another since Acre, as I recall."

"Does the Emperor know all this?"

Leopold looked surprised. "Why, of course, naturally." He spoke too quickly. "I think he may even join us later on in Vienna."

Richard frowned thoughtfully. Leopold's men stared at him curiously: this was the legendary English King. They examined him as if he were a wild beast, a lion.

"I accept your invitation," said Richard finally.

Leopold smiled happily. "You do me a great honor," he said, blushing like a girl.

"Let me arrange a few things," said Richard and he walked towards the bedroom. "Oh, and by any chance do you have some Austrian coin? I'll need to pay the innkeeper."

Leopold giggled and took a purse from one of his attendants and handed it to Richard.

"You will be repaid," said Richard.

"Oh, I expect I shall be," said Leopold.

Richard entered the bedroom. "Here," he whispered to Blondel and he poured half the coins onto the bed. "You'll need these; there's just a chance they won't take you with us. If they don't, go back to England and . . . here, take this ring: Berengaria gave it to me; present it to her and then tell Longchamp everything, that I've been taken prisoner and that he's to pay the ransom as soon as he learns it . . . you understand?"

Blondel nodded. Richard helped him to his feet and embraced him. "Good luck," he whispered. Then he took his heavy cloak and helmet and before Blondel could say a word he was out of the room.

"Ready, Your Majesty?"

"Ready, Leopold. My knight, William of l'Etoug, will come with me, of course."

"Why certainly . . . but wasn't there . . ."

"When did you last see the Emperor?" asked Richard quickly.

"Who? The Emperor? Let me think. A few months ago . . . in October, I believe. Yes, October: I was in Frankfort for a few days."

"How was his health?"

"Oh, very good now. It's quite a healthy family, you know. But naturally you know that since you're related to him."

"We're all related," said Richard dryly.

"Quite true, cousin," said Leopold, smiling. "Shall we leave now?"

"I'll pay the innkeeper first."

Blondel stood balanced against the wall beside the door. Then, shakily, he walked back to the bed and fell across it. He heard the sound of horses' hoofs strike stone. He fainted and, for a long time, existed in a dreamless, mindless place, without Richard, without pain or memory.

THE SEARCH

Winter: 1192–1193

1

The day after the King's capture, Blondel paid the innkeeper, went to a house near the edge of the town and there hid for several days. The town was still full of the Duke's soldiers and he realized how lucky he had been: in the excitement of Richard's capture they *had* forgotten him. But now a proclamation had been read in the square and a reward was being offered for Blondel the troubadour.

He sat by a small fire and made plans; the house belonged to the widow of a blacksmith, a large, strong-boned woman with several children; she had taken him in, been paid liberally, and sworn not to hand him over to the soldiers. He had stayed with her several days. She had treated his back with various herbs and compresses of mud and spider webs, and during the day while she worked in the blacksmith shop, he sat alone by the fire and wondered what next to do.

First, of course, he must get word to England that Richard had been taken prisoner. Should he go himself, though? Certainly someone would have to go and soon. Richard was not expected home for another month, and in a month . . . Blondel refused to think of Richard dead. No, the English would have to know immediately and the sooner they opened negotiations with Leopold and, if necessary, form an army and appeal to the Pope, the better it would be for Richard. Yet, and here he paused in his planmaking, he hadn't the slightest idea where the King was being held or even why: except, obviously, for some sort of ransom. He was safe if Leopold wanted ransom but perhaps, if he tried to escape, they would kill him, and most certainly he would try that. Or perhaps, once the ransom was received, Leopold would have Richard killed and say he died of illness. The possibilities were endless and his head ached thinking of them, aware of his own inadequacy, of his responsibility. What should he do? He stared at the fire but no answer occurred to him: red, blue and yellow flames flickered, answerless.

"You'll have to go today," said the woman. He started; he hadn't known she was in the room.

"I'm ready," he said, glad to be forced into action.

"The soldiers are searching the whole town for you. Tonight or tomorrow they will come here."

"I must go anyway," he said: he spoke a little German now. "You've been kind," he began, awkwardly.

"You can repay me," she said evenly, "with a bit more money and the promise that if they catch you, and they probably will, you'll never mention my name."

He gave her the money and the promise. He smiled as he promised, for he had never known her name.

She had mended his cloak neatly and, a few days earlier,

had bought him a heavy undertunic of wool. At least he would be warm as he walked: his horse had been seized by the Duke's men. He put on his cloak, drawing it tight through the ring brooch. He winced, more from habit than pain, as the heavy cloth fell on his scarred, barely healed shoulders. Thanks to the woman and her herbs his back had healed without infection. He strapped his viol on one shoulder and tied the purse about his neck under the outer tunic. For a moment he held Richard's ring in his hand: it was a heavy gold ring circling, instead of a stone, the Plantagenet arms; then, almost without thinking, he slipped it on his own finger. He would find the King first, he decided, and then, with this news, he would return to England. If he couldn't find the King in a few weeks he would have to send word back by someone else while he continued the search.

Outside the weather was cold but not so cold as it had been; no wind blew and walking warmed him. He stepped immediately upon the road to Vienna: it was near the house and, fortunately, he wouldn't have to cross the town.

There was little traffic on the road. A knight and his squire galloped past. Two priests at a more leisurely pace trotted by and, at a walk, a merchant and his retinue moved slowly towards Vienna. Woods bordered the road and gave him a sense of security: a place to hide.

The road was Roman, he noticed, and he thought of Rome as he walked, wondering how any country could have been so powerful. For instance, no country today had been able to build roads one half so good as those Rome had left like a stone net over Europe. Of course, he could imagine no country controlling all Europe the way Rome had. The German Henry called himself Holy Roman Emperor but, as people were always saying, he was neither holy, nor Roman, nor, on close examination, much of an emperor. Philip, the French King, somewhat optimistically called himself Augustus and was, more or less, heir to Charlemagne but his power was not equal to that of the great Charles and, certainly, not to that of the Caesars. Sometimes he thought that Richard might become the new lord of Europe but he doubted this: he would first have to consolidate his own British islands and this would take a lifetime and might, in the end, perhaps, be impossible. Then he was not sure whether Richard was much interested in political power, in being Caesar. He was more interested in war and money. When he succeeded to the throne, he sold bishoprics, seized estates from nobles he disliked and sold them again for his own profit. For a sum of money he had practically given Scotland to William, also known as the Lion. He'd embarked on his crusade with a clearly conceived vision of personal enrichment and, in this, he had shown more practicality than any of his predecessors. If he thought it practical (and had the means) he might, one day, decide to conquer Europe, but Blondel, who had no illusions about him, knew that he was no statesman in the sense Philip or Henry was, and, when it came to political and diplomatic dealings, Richard would, temperamentally, be at a considerable disadvantage. Richard fought Saracens for treasure and because he liked fighting; empires were seldom made by such men, or, if so made, crumbled usually with the soldier's death.

He breathed the cold air and wondered if he dare sing. No, not here. Someone might hear him and a troubadour singing in French would arouse suspicion. Yet for the first time in weeks he wanted to sing.

The highway followed, for a time, the broad river and Blondel, who thought France the most beautiful of all countries, admitted to himself that this countryside, even in the winter, was beautiful, austere and, in this season, somber. Across the fast-moving brown river were fields and valleys, hills, villages, mountains and castles: a pale fog, blue-white, like smoke lay in the cups of valleys, or like feathers resting: pieces of the winter sky.

Trees grew on the river banks; willows bent and touched the water with unleaved branches. Small boats drifted by, carrying fishermen. He remembered that as a child he used to go out on the Atlantic with his fishermen cousins and he could still recall in detail the hot sun reflected on the bright green sea and the hard brown arms of his cousins as they cast their nets. He longed for that warmth now even though it wasn't unpleasant walking alone in this winter country. Bits of verse came into his head. There was a lady he'd known at Blois . . . what was her name? She'd been the Lady for several ballads and he thought of her again. Perhaps he would make a new ballad as he walked. Words, phrases and rhymes came into his head and he began to hum an experimental tune; then he remembered Richard and he stopped guiltily. He shouldn't be happy now, making ballads. If he were to make a ballad it should be about Richard. What rhymed, he wondered, with Richard?

It was already night when he arrived in Vienna. Even in the darkness he was conscious of a large city, could feel its uneasy breathing about him. The buildings were of many different heights with pointed roofs. The streets were narrow and some were cobbled. People said that Vienna would be the greatest city in Europe one day, larger and more beautiful than either Rome or Paris. And Leopold was said to have great ambitions, for both his city and himself.

The night was foggy and the moon's light diffuse; a dark nascence touched steep roofs. He could see the spires of a large church and, near by, the facade of what appeared to be a palace. Horsemen rode quickly through the streets, clattering on the cobbles. Servants carrying smoky torches lighted the way for courtiers riding in their chairs to important functions, riding on the shoulders of sturdy peasants.

He wandered through the streets, hand always on his sword's hilt, for the streets of any city are dangerous, full of thieves and menace for the stranger, until at last he found an inn. In the old days there were only cookshops and wineshops and travelers slept in the open or in stables or, if they were fortunate, in some noble's castle or a monastery, accepting hospitality if one were rich, charity if one were poor. But now there were places where, for money, one could eat, drink and sleep, sometimes in beds, more often on the floor before a banked fire.

He knocked on a heavy door and the master of the inn opened it and, seeing that he was alone and apparently harmless, let him in. They made arrangements for the night in German.

Then Blondel sat at the end of a long trestle table. A dozen men, all Austrian, sat at the same table eating and drinking noisily; they had stopped when he entered, looked at him curiously and then, satisfied, begun to eat and talk again.

"You troubadour?" asked one heavy man in a loud voice, pronouncing words carefully: the way people do with foreigners.

Blondel touched his viol instinctively and said, yes, he was.

"Sing then," said a rat-faced man, a merchant, for he wore a bit of fur on his cap and his tunic was made of gold cloth beneath wine and grease stains.

"I sing in French only," said Blondel, tearing a piece of mutton with his fingers; he was tired and his legs were sore from walking; his back still hurt him when he thought about it.

"We know some French, enough French," said the rat loftily

"When I finish eating . . . if I may," he added in French; none of them understood. They nodded heavily. When he grew tired of eating, grew warm and comfortable from the fire and the wine, he pulled a stool in front of the fire, at a safe distance for his back was sensitive to heat, and then, idly, he began to play his viol, wondering what to sing: whether to sing an old song or improvise . . . He decided he would sing an old song for to improvise well he needed an appreciative audience, excitement and competition. Softly he began to sing one of his old ballads about the Lady of Blois. It was a long time since he'd sung in a room like this, a room of any kind. His voice was light and resonant. He hadn't the range of Peire Vidal or the tricks of voice of Raimbaud of Vacquerias, but his voice, he knew, had a certain wit, a gentleness which moved men and women equally, could make them weep when he chose: even Austrian merchants.

As he sang of the Lady he wondered which Lady he'd written of in this ballad. The Lady of Blois, he'd thought when he began it, but now he was not so sure: it was a later ballad and the Lady was probably Adclaide. He had loved her for a time: a slim, long-necked woman, very pale with white uneven teeth. Her husband had gone to Italy and Blondel had been, for a time, her constant companion. His ballads told of frustration and continual attendance: they were conventional ballads and not to be taken literally. It was customary to write longingly of the unapproachable Lady whose eyes were remote and pitiless, reflecting ice, bestowing, at most, a flower or a pitying smile, relieving thus the terrible anguish of her articulate lover.

He had known so many Ladies, so many women, and there were few he hadn't known as well as he'd wanted. But for the sake of the form, his medium, the conventional pattern of his art, he wrote of eternal anguish and all the Ladies were flattered, for they appeared the way they would like to be: beautiful, remote and inscrutable, loved. He smiled as he sang, thinking of this. He'd only loved one woman as he remembered, looking back: her name was Marguerite, a girl of nineteen when he was not much older and troubadour at the court of Blois. They had walked together on the banks of the Loire one summer and he had held her hand, sung, improvised for her and she had watched him with dark gray eyes, serene and contented, for to be nineteen and loved is all any woman can demand. Then, the next year she was married to a nobleman in Lorraine and Blondel, though he had always known she would marry and go away, that a peasant like himself couldn't marry her, still, knowing all this, wept often the next summer and walked alone by the river, indifferent to the brilliant green-yellow hills and the singing of birds. He made a number of ballads, though; they were so sad that everyone at court wept happily whenever he sang them.

After that there had been so many Ladies. So many that he had forgotten all but a few, the ones he had made ballads for. They had all been flattered to have a troubadour love them, for troubadours were the most celebrated of men, and even kings, Richard for instance, tried to write ballads and sing them, tried to be troubadours. Richard's ballads were often excellent: well constructed, romantic, but unfortunately he had no voice; he sang a great deal, however, and was much applauded: Nero receiving laurels at Athens.

Now when Blondel sang of love he thought of no one: only of lovemaking, of the idea of separation and of sadness.

He thought even of the King, but as an idea rather than as a person. He thought of gardens and the river Loire, of Picardy, of the castle at Blois and the days when he was young and warm all the time, not cold as he often was now in the life of constant winter he had led since the crusade began: so many Ladies, so many gardens . . . and he found there were tears in his own eyes as he softly sang the *envoi*. *This* was a sign of age.

The Austrians, though they had understood almost nothing, wept contentedly, nevertheless; moved by his voice, by memories they all had or felt they should have; even the rat was convinced that once he had been handsome and, hopelessly, had wooed a cold princess. They asked for more, and Blondel, in a mood of firelight and rhyming, sang of the spring in France and, singing, forgot winter and a strange and hostile city.

After a while he grew tired and stopped and, though they begged, he refused to sing any more and he sat there, still and sad, sadder even than his own ballads.

A man came up behind him and said in Norman French, "Aren't you Richard's troubadour? aren't you Blondel?"

He looked up and saw a tall blond man, dressed in the robes of a pilgrim, covering, Blondel was certain, a suit of mail. "Yes," he said, surprising himself, trusting the other. "And you?"

"An English knight, returning from Palestine."

"Sit down," said Blondel, motioning to a place on the floor beside him. There was a slight metallic clash as the man arranged himself on the floor. Blondel glanced about the room and saw that the Austrians were busy with their own affairs: some drinking, others preparing to sleep on the benches or the floor . . . none noticed the two by the fire.

"Have you heard the news?" asked Blondel.

"Only rumors . . . what happened?"

The Englishman was astonished when he heard. "But how did they dare touch him? why would Leopold seize him? There'll be a war."

Blondel shrugged: "Ransom, and there is an old feud; besides, I think, the Emperor ordered it."

"Were you with him when it happened? with Richard?"

"Yes," and Blondel described what had happened. The English knight sighed when he finished. "Now John will be King and that's the end of us all. Richard was the ideal Norman King: he never visited England but John will never leave it."

"Richard isn't dead yet," said Blondel sharply.

"He'd be better off dead if he doesn't go back to England soon. I've heard that Longchamp has been deposed and that John's governing and that he's made an alliance with Philip; oh, he hasn't wasted any time while his brother was away."

"Stories get exaggerated this far from England." But he was afraid.

"Perhaps."

"You have a horse?" asked Blondel.

"Certainly."

"Then I want you to deliver a message to Queen Eleanor; will you?"

The knight nodded. "I'm not for John."

Blondel found a bit of parchment in his wallet and then, with a pointed piece of charcoal from the fire, he described briefly, in Latin, Richard's capture and the beginning of his own search. Finished, he took Richard's ring, rubbed charcoal on the coat-of-arms and pressed it, like a seal, beneath his own signature. He gave the message to the knight, who placed it in his wallet.

"I'll be in Normandy in a few days. Where shall I find the Queen?"

"I don't know, but you will find her." They slept side by side before the fire and Blondel, in spite of the soreness of his back, slept well. In the morning when he woke he found the English knight gone; he wished he had asked his name.

He walked in the streets of Vienna that day, listening to gossip in the taverns. He followed nobles in the street, trying to overhear their conversations. Finally, hearing nothing but trivial gossip, the prices and opinions of the day, he went to a church. The priest, a serene, cordial man, learning that he was French and recently arrived from Palestine, talked with him awhile. So he was a troubadour. Good troubadours were popular in Austria. Leopold especially liked them. Where was the Duke? Well, just this morning he had heard that the Duke was on his way to the castle at Tiernstein, some distance from Vienna. There was also a curious rumor that the Lion-Heart was his guest or, some claimed, prisoner. There was probably no truth in this since everyone knew of the trouble at Acre and, since there'd been trouble, why would Richard come to Austria? Still, only this morning he had been told . . .

2

If he'd had the money he would certainly have bought a horse and if he'd had the opportunity he would certainly have stolen one, but lacking both opportunity and money, he walked.

The days were still cold but fortunately there was little wind and much of his way took him through forests, dark

Austrian forests which had a weather of their own, different from the open country where men lived.

He saw few people in the forests, for peasants were afraid of the evil spirits and the thieves who lived in the dragon-haunted, giant-frequented darkness, among the silent corridors between old trees. But evil spirits never touched him and the only thieves he saw wanted him to stay with them and sing since there was no music in the forest.

The road to Tiernstein, a broad and rutted highway in open country, became a footpath in the forest. He walked, humming to himself, wondering what it would be like to do a ballad about the forest in winter, comparing his blighted heart to the winter: or was that too obvious? "Black trees like fingers in the ice" . . . "frozen birds in the branches" . . . "turned to ice in flight" . . . "cry of wolves" . . . Then he forgot about the ballad and thought seriously of wolves. This was, of course, the season for them and he was alone in a forest inhabited solely, he was sure, by wolves. He looked about him as he walked, for some sign, a track . . . but the ground was too hard and, besides, he was safe during the day. At night he would sleep in the branches of a tree.

That night the moon became full; he could see it shining round and curiously dingy-looking, held upon the sharp tips of two trees, a phantom's skull on two spears.

He made his fire, grew warm. Behind him was a tree with large comparatively comfortable-looking branches. He would, at least, be able to climb it easily, like a ladder. He hadn't climbed a tree since he was a child in Picardy, and the trees of his childhood were bright, different from these sinister shapes; perhaps all the Austrian forests were cities transformed by magic, cursed by sorcerers, waiting for princes, deaths of dragons and the awakening of tower-guarded princesses.

As he ate his dinner he heard, as he knew he would, the high sound of wolves calling in the forest. He put more wood on his fire; he could already see, or imagine he saw, red eyes looking at him from the darkness, luminous as fire. He climbed into his tree; two large branches grew close together and he arranged himself upon them, his cloak wrapped tightly about him and his sword half drawn. He was barely warmed by the fire below him. Shivering, he closed his eyes and tried to sleep but every time a wolf howled he started; he decided that after this night he would sleep by day and travel in the night; awake, he felt he could take his chances with the wolves.

He must have slept awhile for, when he started suddenly, he found his body was stiff and cramped; like an animal he had sensed danger. The moon-skull had rolled off the spears, out of sight: rolling, no doubt, down black hills, over the rim of the earth. His fire was almost out; only a few embers glowed. He was cold and his back was sore from pressing against the rough bark. He was changing his position when a wolf howled so near him that he almost lost his balance. He drew his sword and, in so doing, did lose his balance: he fell out of the tree, sword in hand, and landed, with a jolt, on his feet. He looked about him but saw nothing, not even eyes. Perhaps the cry had been farther away than he thought: sound carried far in an empty winter forest.

Then he heard someone behind him; he turned and saw a man standing at the foot of the tree. The man was thickly built, muscular, with a long graying beard. He wore a tunic made of the pelts of wolves.

"Who are you?" asked Blondel in German, his voice unsteady.

"Since you're the trespasser I must ask you that. Who are you?" said the other.

61

. "Blondel, a French troubadour, returning from the Holy Land." All this said quickly, ingenuously, deflecting with truth all menace.

"A troubadour?" The man glanced speculatively at Blondel's viol.

"And you?" asked Blondel.

"Stefan . . . king of the werewolves."

Blondel wondered whether if he fainted everything might, perhaps, disappear like a dream: the forest, the night, the werewolf . . .

Stefan smiled. "Yes, there are many of us in these forests. But instead of eating human flesh we live on gold taken from human visitors."

This was better. He could deal with thieves. "I've no gold," he began.

"But you can sing. Come," said Stefan, and obediently Blondel followed him. They walked only a short distance: the lair was near by. It was a cave set in a small hill. A heavy wooden door, reinforced with metal, stood open. Blondel noticed that vines were draped over the door and, when shut, the door disappeared into the side of the hill. They entered the cave and Blondel found himself in a large hall of earth with wooden pillars holding up the low ceiling; at one end of the room a fire burned on a platform of stone, a hole in the earth-ceiling drew the smoke out of the cave. A table ran the width of the room and, on benches before the table, sat the werewolf bandits, all dressed, like their chief, in the skins of wolves. Eating and talking loudly, they looked suspiciously at Blondel but did nothing since he was with Stefan. At the end of the room, on a dais, was Stefan's chair with a table in front of it. Stefan motioned to one of several boys who waited on the men at their table. "Bring a stool for the troubadour and food for us both." He turned to

Blondel. "It's almost sunrise," he said, "and time to sleep. We hunted many hours tonight."

"With success?"

"Oh, yes. The hunting's always good in our forest," and he motioned to the carcass of a deer being roasted over the fire.

"You live on the forest, then?"

"And travelers." Stefan smiled and Blondel noticed with alarm that his teeth were yellow and pointed. Could men really become wolves? Was it possible that he might suddenly find himself surrounded by wolves in this cave? He shuddered and Stefan, seeing this, laughed and said, "Only rich travelers interest us; abbots and priests, merchants with baggage trains and nobles who travel with too few guards. Robbery is generally a daytime task since now, for fear of wolves, so few people travel by night in my forest."

The boy placed a stool in front of the table and Blondel sat down opposite Stefan. Another boy brought venison and wine. The plates were of heavy silver and the goblets gold. "The property," said Stefan fingering his goblet, "of a prince of the Church. I like to think sometimes that the Holy Father himself might have drunk from this goblet," and he crossed himself piously at the thought.

When they had eaten Stefan showed Blondel about the hall, showed him the bolted doors to treasure chambers, to passages which ran beneath the forest floor. In case of a direct attack on their cave, the werewolves could disappear into the earth in a moment. Most of their treasure was not kept here anyway, he remarked. The men were gathered about the fire now, dicing and drinking. "All right, troubadour," said Stefan, "pay for your supper." And Blondel took his viol and played for them. He forgot everything as he sang, forgot the werewolves and his danger, forgot even the imprisoned King.

Then when he grew tired at last and wanted to stop, the men shouted for more and he sang until, finally, his voice grew hoarse and, through the open door, he could see the forest turning white with morning. He stopped at last, was permitted to stop, and the men slept on the floor, wrapped in their furs, the great fire hissing and crackling, a sleepy guard at the door, the table littered with bones and spilt wine.

"Stay with us," said Stefan. They were the only two awake in the hall.

"I can't," said Blondel and he told him of Richard's capture.

Stefan nodded as he spoke and showed no surprise. "We'd already heard of it in the forest. Leopold and a large party passed through here on their way to Tiernstein. Someone said that the Lion-Heart was with him." Stefan sighed. "I've often wished the Duke would pass through here with a *small* party . . . but he always has an army with him." Stefan got up and walked over to one of a number of chests behind his chair. He opened it and took out a silver medallion on a chain. He handed it to Blondel. "Take this," he said. "It's the pentagram, our sign. It will take you safely through any forest in Austria."

Blondel thanked him and put the chain about his neck. "You'll never be able to find your way back here," said Stefan, "but should you ever come through my forest again and one of my men stops you, tell him to bring you here. Music is good for us, troubadour; we miss such things in here." Stefan showed his yellow teeth thoughtfully; then, "Come, I'll show you the road to Tiernstein."

A few winter birds chattered among the bare branches. A stag watched them for an instant, then fled. The air was cold and smelled of moss and damp stone, of wood and

woodsmoke. They found the path again and Blondel, looking about him, was surprised to find that he had no idea
from which direction he'd come.

"Good-bye," said Stefan and he embraced Blondel hearti-
ly. "There's the road to Tiernstein." Blondel glanced at the
road before him, a faint trail across the forest. Then he
turned to say good-bye to Stefan but he was already gone.

The castle stood, harsh, unornamented, on a hill. The
castles of Austria were not much different from the Norman
except they were often more massive, designed to hold back
not only the warring armies of Christian kings but also the
barbarians: the vast heathen tribes of Asia who, from time to
time, swept down upon Europe, looting and killing.

The captain of the guard greeted Blondel more warmly than
guards usually greet strangers. He was a slim and handsome
man, with straight blond hair the color of silver and blue-
violet eyes.

"A troubadour! We could really have used you last week,
but enter, enter. From France? The best troubadours are
French, I always say. We see too few of them here at
Tiernstein. Vienna's the place for all that. You've just come
from there? through the forest? alone? That takes courage;
this is the country of werewolves, you know: werewolves and
thieves. You were lucky you saw neither." He led Blondel
into a guard's room near the gate and they sat down on a
bench.

"How long do you expect to stay here? just traveling? Yes,
I know what it's like to want to travel in foreign countries, to
be hundreds, thousands of miles from the people you've
always known. I'd love to see Italy. Have you been there?
They say that in the south it never grows cold, that snow
never falls. I should like that. Shall I speak French? can you

understand me? Good. Strange that people should have different languages and be separated by words." The captain of
the guard thought of this a moment and his face was sad, the
face of one of the Nordic gods, beautiful yet curiously weak:
a god whose strength had been dissipated when his people
turned to Christianity, no longer put flowers on his altar.

"You'll spend some time here," he said, almost pleading.
"You'll sing for us, of course. We hear music so seldom, only
the barking of peasant singers and occasional troubadours,
generally old with cracked voices. Your voice isn't cracked: I
can tell that and, of course, you're young. You've come from
Palestine? I was there for a time but I had to leave before
Acre fell. That's the only life for a man, though: armies and
some cause or other. But pain is bad," he ran a pale muscular hand through his silver hair. "It would be perfect if there
was no pain in battles. A man loses a fight and he turns to
smoke, no blood, no entrails dangling . . . no screams." He
shivered and Blondel, tired and hungry as he was, listened
nevertheless, and recalled, too, the way the parapets of Acre
had looked the morning after Richard had seized the
citadel. "Yes, the pain's the worst thing. You troubadours
never sing of that, though. I suppose you couldn't since
there's no music to go with words like that, with a song of
pain." He scratched his neck thoughtfully; Blondel noticed
coarse blond hair curling at the neck of his tunic, contra-
dicting in some strange way the silver hair of his head. "But
still the life in armies is the pleasantest for a man . . . next to
a life like yours. In the armies a man never feels alone; your
life is different, of course, completely alone, but there's a
freedom to it, and then, it must be wonderful to make up
songs and sing them." The captain of the guard looked at
him and smiled: his teeth were white and even, almost the
whitest teeth Blondel had ever seen on a grown man. "But as

I said you should have come a week ago when we had our Duke here, Leopold. He has good taste in music . . ."

"The Duke has gone?"

"Yes, day before yesterday. To Frankfort, I think; or maybe back to Vienna. There's some sort of crisis going on now and they say he has to meet with the Emperor soon. I hope they're planning a new crusade."

"They say King Richard's his prisoner," said Blondel, deciding to be direct.

The captain frowned, "Where did you hear that?"

"Oh, in Vienna . . . everyone's talking about it."

"I suppose nothing in the world's a secret," said the young captain irritably. "Richard was the Duke's guest. After all, he's a King and we're not at war with England; how could he be the Duke's prisoner?"

"Was he here with the Duke?"

"Yes, he was here."

"What sort of man is he?" asked Blondel quickly, trying to sound idly curious yet at the same time not really interested.

"Very strong-looking with a square face: a large nose, rather light for a Norman. He was very . . ." he paused and squinted as though to recall more clearly some memory, some picture in his mind.

"I was supposed to sing for him once just after the fall of Acre," said Blondel eagerly, playing his part. "I was to sing for him but he disagreed with King Philip, you know, and then, of course, I couldn't. That was just before Philip went back to France."

"They say he's got almost no control over himself. He's supposed to have killed Conrad of Montferrat. Not that it was any great loss to the world . . . But here we talk about all these things when you must be tired from your trip through the forest. Oh, to be able to go anywhere . . . to walk through forests and see the Italian cities." He got to his feet. "I'll show you where you can eat and sleep and then, tonight, you'll sing for us. I'll tell the Lord of Tiernstein you're here. What's your name?"

"Raimond of Toulouse," said Blondel, prepared for the question: Raimond was a celebrated singer, a friend of his who, happily, had not gone to Palestine and he was sure that no one at Tiernstein had ever seen him. But they would know his songs.

"You mean the famous Raimond?"

Blondel smiled modestly and nodded, wondering what effect his own name would have had on the young man; unfortunately he would probably never know. The captain was delighted and introduced himself as Otto. "This will be a great occasion for Tiernstein," he said. He glanced at Blondel's worn tunic. "I'll get you some clothes, too," he said.

There was a murmur of excitement when Blondel, wearing a tunic of blue and yellow, entered the great hall, his silver chain about his neck (the medallion hidden, however). He had refused to meet the Lord and Lady of Tiernstein before he'd sung. Long ago he'd learned the value of dramatic entrances. During dinner he had sat in one of the small rooms off the great hall.

Otto wandered in and out, telling him how many people were in the hall (two hundred, mostly guests who had been invited to attend the Duke and had now, as guests so often will, stayed a few days longer than their invitation). Otto brought him food and offered him wine, which he never drank before he sang. Otto's face was bright with excitement. At last, at the Lord of Tiernstein's command, Blondel walked slowly into the great hall, walked between the rows of tables to the dais, where at a smaller table sat the Lord and Lady and several of the more important guests.

The Lord of Tiernstein was hugely fat. He had two chins, half-moons of flesh suspended under his own original chin. His face was purple-white and his eyes stood out like a frog's; even his voice was a bit like a frog's croak, hoarse, resonant. He fingered the gold chains about his neck as he welcomed Blondel.

"Welcome, Raimond of Toulouse, to our castle." He croaked in heavily accented French. "It would please us if you sang."

Blondel bowed deeply and addressed himself, as was usual, to the Lady of the castle. She was as thin as the Lord was fat. Her breasts were flat, much smaller than her husband's. Her face was sallow and she wore an elaborate gold diadem about her head veil. She was dressed in green shot with gold, a color which made her face the color of an old cheese. Her mouth was wide with a protruding jaw and her eyes were unusually aware and watchful.

He made them a little speech, looking directly at her the whole time, and he almost laughed when she looked modestly at her plate, avoiding his eyes.

Blondel sang and when he finished they applauded loudly. For his final song he improvised a ballad dedicated to the Beauty of Tiernstein, who, listening to his song, turned quite orange with pleasure, her hands flitting helplessly about her person as though to assure herself, by touch, of the beauty the troubadour described. The Lord, well pleased, handed Blondel a purse and told him he might remain at Tiernstein as long as he liked.

Blondel was preparing himself for bed when Otto appeared. "I never heard such singing," he said enthusiastically, "not even in Vienna." Blondel smiled politely as Otto went on, telling him what an effect he had made on everyone, how every woman in the castle was in love with him. Like all troubadours and most men, Blondel enjoyed praise and he accepted young Otto's admiration gracefully, with pleasure.

They talked for an hour and Blondel's yawns were unnoticed; he was wondering whether he should ask Otto to go and let him sleep when the curtain of his door was pulled aside and a woman, a servant from her dress, said mysteriously, with no explanation, "Come with me."

Blondel looked questioningly at Otto, who sighed unhappily, nodded and said, "I'll see you in the morning." The servant led him across the great hall; coals glowed, reddening the darkness, casting shadows. Servants, sleeping on the floor, providing an unconscious audience for a play of shadows.

At the end of a gallery, they came to a wooden door which the servant pushed open. For a moment Blondel blinked in the brightness. Then he saw a large apartment, many candles, two deep windows, furs upon the floor, a much-carved bed and, standing in the center of this room, the Lady of Tiernstein, wearing a simple, tight-fitting white tunic which showed to wonderful disadvantage her peculiar figure.

"Do come in, Raimond," she said in excellent French. "I felt, after this evening, that it would be wrong of me not to receive you. I know how you young men are . . . especially troubadours," and she giggled.

He bowed, wondering what to say. "I'm overwhelmed, my lady."

"Come sit beside me." She led him to a bench which could seat only two people and those two not comfortably unless they were lovers.

"Now tell me all about your travels, Raimond," she said,

one of her long fluttering hands touching his sleeve, his shoulder, nervously.

"There's so much to tell," he said uncomfortably and then, to be confusing, added, "and so little."

"Oh, how I hated that merciless lady you sang about tonight!" exclaimed the compassionate Lady of Tiernstein. "She must have had no heart at all. How different I'd have been if I were her!" She giggled again, a high thin noise like the shriek of a mouse.

This was going to be very disagreeable, thought Blondel. Either he would have to go through with this seduction or else he would have to leave Tiernstein tonight. The thought of another night in the woods was not pleasant but, glancing at the lady, neither was this. Then he remembered why he had come to Tiernstein, that he still had no information of Richard: perhaps there would be a miracle yet and he would be saved.

"So few women have a heart, my lady," he said softly, not looking at her face.

"But not all of us, dear Raimond, are so cold. Some of us will give everything, even," and she paused, "even our virtue, for a loving man."

"So few, my lady, have such charity, such goodness," said Blondel, wondering desperately if he could ever get the conversation around to Richard, to anything else. He felt the pressure of a bony knee against his; slowly, with great care, he moved his own knee away.

"I . . . I was sorry, my lady," he said, making the transition as delicately as possible, "that I could not sing for the Duke and Richard."

"Oh . . . yes, they would have enjoyed listening to you. Call me Hedwig, Raimond."

"What sort of man was Richard?"

71

"Well . . ." this new topic obviously didn't interest her. "Impetuous, very romantic . . . I was terribly embarrassed because he wooed me in front of my husband. Imagine! I was honored, of course, but I could never have hoped to return his love even though he was a king." She smiled virtuously; her teeth were bad.

"He went back to Vienna with the Duke, didn't he?"

"Yes, they went on to Vienna together. I expect he'll be the Duke's guest for quite some time." Now he knew and now he could leave. They talked a few moments longer: she discussing the relative merits of different women's hearts and he indicating sadly a long faithfulness to a lady in Provence. Then he rose to go.

"I can't control myself much longer," he said, tensely, simulating passion under control. "But you know I can't stay; I don't trust myself." Now that he was going he would perform a little, if only out of relief. "I have too great a respect for my lady's station, for her virtue, and I must respect the hospitality of my lord. Besides," and he touched his chest, moved by the fervor, the obviousness of his own performance, "I have sworn to love no woman until my lady in Provence receives me." He stopped, not daring to look at her, waiting.

When he finally looked up again he saw she was standing in front of him, a curious expression on her yellow face. "If you leave this room now," she said and her voice was determined, "I will go immediately to my husband and tell him you forced your way into my apartments and attacked me."

Blondel, astonished and dismayed, stood quite still for a minute and then, almost amused, smiled and said, "I'll certainly stay, my lady."

She giggled, mouselike, and said, coyly, softly, "Shall we talk about love, troubadour?"

"By all means . . . Hedwig," said Blondel, briskly; and he wondered often in the course of that dreadful night if any king had ever been so well served as Richard was by him.

3

The next day he presented himself to the Lord of Tiernstein and told him that he must, regretfully, continue his pleas- antly interrupted journey back to France. The great lord was understanding and nodded gravely, losing his original chin in the purple flesh of the half-moons. "You must visit us again, troubadour," he said.

Blondel turned to the Lady of Tiernstein. "I shall always remember your courtesy, kindness and beauty," he said cer- emoniously.

Hedwig, with a contented smile, gave him her hand. She was relaxed, serene this morning: the long hands for once still. "You have given us great pleasure, Raimond of Toulouse," she said formally, her wide mouth set in a smile.

Then Otto led him sadly to the gate. "You saw old Hedwig, didn't you?" Blondel nodded, surprised to hear him speak so bitterly of the lady of his castle. Otto kicked the ground viciously, scuffing the dirt with his boot. "I should have known she'd get you," he said. "If I'd warned you, you could have slept with the men-at-arms. She wouldn't have been able to send for you in front of all of them. Not that she hasn't been through the whole garrison at one time or another."

"You, too?"

Otto shook his head, "No, I'm Tiernstein's nephew, his favorite you might say, and so she's never really dared do anything with me. You know she's one of the reasons I liked

Richard when he was here. After dinner, the first night, a few of us were in the Duke's apartments and she was flirting, very discreetly for her, with the King when, suddenly, he announced that the only women he liked were young pretty peasant girls, and he looked at her the whole time he was talking and I thought she would run out of the room." Otto laughed and put his arm through Blondel's. "I'd really hoped you would be able to stay here for a while. I wanted to talk to you about so many things," he said wistfully. Blondel smiled and looked at him. His back hurt and he wondered if Hedwig had noticed the scars; they were sore this morning. She had said nothing about them. He must *really* think of something else, of what Otto was saying.

"I've a friend, Stefan of Dreisen; he's about my age and one of the Duke's knights; I hope you'll see him in Vienna. He's at court and I'm sure you'll like him. He could present you to the Duke if you wanted to sing at court." They were now at the gate. The sun shone yellow and the sky was an icy blue and cloudless; in the sun the day was warm. Blondel took a deep breath; he almost looked forward to the trip back to Vienna.

"Well . . . good-bye," said Otto, taking Blondel's hand in both of his. "Maybe we'll see each other again." Blondel saw that he was really moved.

"I hope so, Otto," and he was surprised how warmly he felt about this young man, unhappy in these Austrian forests, removed from the warm countries he himself had always known and for which, he knew, the other longed.

They shook hands and Blondel turned and walked down the hill from the castle. He glanced back only once and saw that Otto was still standing in the gateway, watching him.

Day followed day and he moved across forests and open country, between mountains and over hills. As he walked he had no sense of urgency; the rhythm of his body in motion limited his awareness to the instant and he seldom realized that he was moving towards some event which could not be anticipated, though the fact of it was known and existed always in the unconscious part of his mind. But he did understand as he walked that the events of the moment were important and that what might happen was not, for it had no existence yet: the shape of the future remained strange and formless in his mind. He could only be positive that he would, in the future, die, and the actual reality of that, its shape and its meaning, could not, certainly, be anticipated nor, for a moment, comprehended. And so he moved across the land in winter, moved towards a city and, moving, thought of his past in irrelevant fragments; a past that existed only as memory in the single reality of the present: a vague world of deeds performed in a place where castles, landscapes and even faces were often obscure, confused; where a room might be complete but for its ceiling, say, or the face of a childhood friend complete except for a nose and eyes: so much forgotten, so much that never was. But he recalled what he could of what had happened. And, living in the present, but allowing it to merge with the vague world of events recalled, he kept himself from thoughts of death, of the future: the moment when the heart would flutter sickeningly and the last short breath would strangle in his throat; not until that had happened would past and present and future become one thing for an instant, one moment of all time and then: nothing beyond time. But now he was alive and he thought of his life in France, in England, in Palestine. He had traveled so much and at such speed; on the swiftest horses, on fast ships, but now he walked alone, trying to find a friend imprisoned in some castle as yet unknown, a friend who, for all he knew, might now be dead; damp earth pressed on the blue eyes.

Time ceased to disturb him as he was caught up in the rhythm of his moving body: he was contented to have no one to talk to, no conflict with the world: he was timeless, in motion. He ate; slept; he made fires. Sometimes he sang to himself and sometimes he talked to himself, reliving certain scenes, playing them over again to his own advantage, and thus, easily, he changed the shape of the past, pressed the amorphous memories into pleasant shapes. In time, he realized that the past was only what he chose to make it: his personal kingdom where he was the master and where he reigned. He allowed his memory to drift as it pleased: Blois and this woman; Cyprus and that woman; Acre and a quarrel . . . the days with Richard. He had so many things to recall if he chose. He walked, singing to himself: a being, momentarily divorced from time, separate from the world: he existed now and that was enough; he moved, a single star from darkness to darkness falling.

One evening he came to a village. A few small houses, a stone shrine for a church, a crossroads of frozen earth and that was all, no castle, no fortifications. The people of this village worked the land for a lord who lived some distance away.

"You are welcome to stay here," said the owner of the largest house, a white-haired peasant, bowing with great dignity, slipping the coin Blondel had given him into his own purse.

That night Blondel sat with the family about a wooden table and they asked him questions of the outside world; none of them had ever seen a city; none had even traveled the short distance to Vienna.

The peasant's wife, an old woman, was a feminine version

of her husband. They had two sons, grown men, large-muscled with fair silky hair and beards: they were simple, good young men, still not married but, he learned, soon to be. The old couple's niece waited on them while they were at table, and afterwards she sat on a stool near the end of the table and listened to Blondel. She was a pretty girl with pale hair, lighter even than her cousins', almost like the white hair of her uncle and aunt. She wore it in two long braids; her tunic was blue and she wore no veil, no elaborate gir-dle . . . she reminded him of the girls he'd known as a boy in Picardy: simple, animal girls who laughed a great deal, made love, married, had children and quickly lost their prettiness and their laughter. But this girl was not quite like them; she acted differently: she was quiet and smiled seldom; when she spoke her voice was low, not high and sharp the way the voices of peasant girls so often are; of great ladies, too, for that matter, he thought, recalling Hedwig of Tiernstein. This girl's face even as she listened to his stories of Acre was seri-ous, relaxed. Her features were small and regular and her skin was light, a pearl reflecting firelight. Her hands were short, he noticed, and red from working in the cold.

"Have you really seen the Lion-Heart?" she asked sudden-ly in a low voice, her first remark that evening.

"Oh, yes, many times; I've sung for him, too." He smiled at her.

"What sort of man is he? I . . . we've heard he's the bravest man that ever lived." Her uncle looked at her sternly; it was not proper for her to talk so much, especially to a stranger. She ignored him, however.

"He's very brave," said Blondel, wondering which of sev-eral stories to tell. "I once saw him take two armed Saracens, lift them off the ground and throw them at two more who stood guarding a parapet; all four fell over the parapet. Oh, he was like a lion at Acre. You could hear his voice from one end of the battle to the other. He rode a black horse into that battle and you could tell he was the King just by the way he looked, and that's not common, for kings generally look like other men. But that day Richard looked as tall as a tower and there were times when I thought fire and smoke would come out of his mouth instead of words. I remember him now, shouting and swearing, riding up a narrow street with only a handful of men, the rest of his army far behind. A hundred Saracens waited at the top of the street and he killed them all: blood flowed in the streets and his sword smoked . . ."

Blondel was carried away by his own stories; he could almost see, as he talked, that hot fierce day when the sun made their armor feel like molten metal burning their skins; he remembered the stench of the dead all covered with flies, armies and armies of flies. But when one speaks of heroes, flies and heat mean nothing, and for that matter, he was sure they'd meant nothing to Richard, intent as he had been on the fighting and the killing: a war god and merciless. He had been magnificent that day and everyone who had seen him was awed and would recall, as Blondel did now, the fury and the splendor, forgetting the flies, the heat, forgetting the shouts and screams: the music such men as Richard make.

He stayed with the old peasant's family for several days: all sense of urgency, for the time, gone. He helped the family build a shed for their pigs even though, ordinarily, he hated to work with his hands; but he was strong and he could work. He'd never been good with his hands, though; worse even than Richard. He smiled when he remembered Richard fixing the innkeeper's spit the day of his capture.

He talked with the niece, Amelia, and he was careful not

to appear too interested, for already he had noticed her aunt watching them.

One night a dance was held in a neighbor's house, a country ritual dance, older than history and, from the sound of the music, almost as old as music itself; he went with his host's family to the dance. Much wine was drunk and almost all the village danced to the noise of several local musicians.

When he had tired of dancing he sat with Amelia on a bench at the back of the room, a dark place where young couples sat, and, moved by the wine, he put his arm around her and noticed how quickly she was breathing; yet her face was serene, though flushed a little from dancing. They were hidden from the rest of the room by a sweaty young man and his girl, sprawled in front of them.

"Let's go back to the house," Blondel whispered. She nodded. They slipped out the back of the house and, unaware of the cold, they walked hand in hand through the bright dead moonlight to her uncle's house. It was still early and they had hours before them. Neither of them thought how strange it would look to her family when it was discovered the two of them had left together, early. Everything was simple, guided by dream logic and desire; complete, yet a little sad, as these things always are or as troubadours say they are.

They talked awhile; still touching one another.

"You know I'll have to leave soon," he said.

"Yes, I know that." She was sad but nothing more. "This is what I've always wanted," she said, finally, so softly he could barely hear her. "It should happen once like this, I think. Now I can marry one of the village boys and have children and be like all the other women here except I'll be able to think about this." She sighed. Then: "But I'll be happy when I think of this."

For an instant he wondered if he should take her with him, take her back to France.

She knew he was thinking this for she said, "I'll always have to stay here. I'm much happier being what I was intended to be yet having something to remember, a difference in my life. Will you leave tomorrow?"

"You want me to go?"

"Yes. I want you to go: the memory's made."

"Yes, I'll go." Then, after a long time, across the darkness of their own making, a light fell. They parted, frightened. Blondel fumbled with his tunic in the dark room. The light had come from the small window, light from a torch outside; now he heard the uncle's voice at the door. His heart almost stopped. He held his tunic against his body and waited for the roof to crash about his head. The uncle stood in the door peering at them; his wife watched them over his shoulder: she smiled grimly.

Amelia managed everything. She told them Blondel would marry her, that they were in love, that he would take her with him to France, that he would give the uncle a fine present of money and demand no dowry. He could hardly hear her voice above the loud and drumlike beating of his heart.

A bit warily the uncle congratulated him and, finally, he was allowed to dress and sleep. Since the brothers slept by the door he couldn't escape that night.

The next morning was one of the most unpleasant of his life. The brothers congratulated him sincerely and welcomed him into their family, and the old woman even smiled at him once, looking at him speculatively. The uncle was cordial but watchful, by no means convinced. Then the young men and their father went off to work on their shed and Amelia and Blondel were left in the house with the old woman. Amelia led him to a corner of the room where the aunt, who was watching them, could hear nothing. "Now you can go," she said. "Run for the crossroads: one leads through the forest, another leads back to the place you came from; the third takes you into the hills: follow that road. They say there's a giant in the hills; perhaps there is and perhaps there isn't, but anyway my uncle would never dare follow you; none of the villagers ever go into those hills."

He held her hand a moment and she smiled. "Now it's done," she said.

Quickly he went to the door and, the surprised shriek of the aunt in his ears, he ran towards the crossroads. He didn't dare look back until, winded and exhausted, he stood on the first of the giant's hills. He looked down and saw the village below him. Amelia stood in front of her house and, closer to him, he saw three men, the angry kinsmen, standing at the crossroads, watching him. He waved to Amelia and, free at last, he descended the hill on the other side.

Again he traveled but now he was less contented than before; he had spent too long a time in the village; he walked quickly, guiltily, to make up for the time lost as he moved again towards Vienna and the King. The way through these hills was the most difficult way to the city and this, in a sense, made him glad, an atonement.

The hills were covered with small bare trees whose thin branches made a brown net through which the clear light of winter shone, white and cold. Between the hills were stony valleys and frozen streams, narrow strips of ice which, in another season, would be swollen rivers of ice fragments and rain from the hills. A cold wind blew in the woods, freezing the hairs of his nostrils, making his face burn.

He followed the trail, passed caves in the rocky cliffs where no doubt werewolves lived, and other and to him more frightening creatures. Yet he though mostly of Amelia as he moved through danger towards danger; a strange girl: he wondered how such an odd wise woman could have been born in this wild country, this country of stolid men and giggling women. Of course, anything could happen anywhere. In the western courts he had known a few women like her but, certainly, not many. Had she come from a western court she would have been able to read or, if not able to read, she would at least have learned of love from gossip and the ballads of troubadours. But not many women, even with these advantages, were as wise as she, as capable of decision or of loving. When the women of the West found a man who pleased them there was, for the man, no escape without scenes, threats and violence. Well, there were two unusual women in Austria he knew of: Hedwig and Amelia, both women of decision, and one, at least, had left him with a pleasant memory. Perhaps some day . . . and almost seriously he thought of returning to the village and taking her back to France with him. He would teach her how to be a lady of the court: Galatea; and he would have Richard give him a title so that she could have it. She would wear beautiful clothes and everyone at the Norman and English courts would envy him for having a wise as well as a lovely wife. He dreamed as he walked of what his life with Amelia would be. They would go from Blois to Paris to Chinon to London. But then, he remembered, a woman couldn't travel the way a troubadour did, couldn't sleep in the open or in peasant's houses. Amelia the peasant girl, perhaps, but not Amelia the countess. It was too difficult; yes, she had been right. Better to meet someone for an instant, to hold another body close to one's own, to be, for an instant, a single creature, part of another with a similar will, and then to part, to desert this magic for ordinary living and a search for the King, equipped thus with only pleasant memory, separating before boredom has destroyed the magic in one's arms, before the sad awakening that one has touched another person, a separate being and unknown. So much better to go from lover to lover, from instant to instant, performing the ritual of completion and then, with new memory, go walking again in the clear air of a winter day, remembering only the enchantment, the complemented rhythm of another's body, existing at last as personal fantasy, unshared and, finally, possessed: a memory of fire and constant as fire is not. She had been right to make him go. She would have her memory now for all her life and he would remember, too, for a time.

Now he must think of his journey and her warning. He had heard of giants all his life. He had known men who had seen giants as tall as cathedrals, they claimed, and he had always doubted their stories. He had always doubted what he had never seen: giants, dragons, witches, the lives of the saints and the resurrection of Christ. But now, having once seen a dragon, he was more prepared than he'd ever been before to believe in the exceptional.

An hour before nightfall when the sky was twilight gray and the wind had gone, the branches still, he passed through a gorge, boulder-strewn, and here, standing on a rock, was the tallest man he had ever seen.

"Stop," said the giant; his voice was thin. He was half again as tall as an ordinary man, as Blondel. A man's head could have been hidden in one of his hands. He wore an old and filthy tunic; his beard was matted and he looked like an early Christian martyr, magnified somewhat.

"Who are you, trespasser?" asked the giant, climbing slowly and awkwardly down from his rock until he stood in front of Blondel, looking down at him. He was filthy, thought

Blondel who was usually not disturbed by such things; fright kept him from running, made him stand there and think how filthy this giant was. "I . . . I'm Raimond," he said at last, "a troubadour from Toulouse."

"A troubadour?" The giant appeared interested; he stopped scowling. "Then you must stop with me," he said with surprising graciousness. "I live close by in one of the caves. Rather rustic, certainly, but I find it comfortable; here, follow me." He led Blondel among the rocks. "By the way, would you rather talk French or Latin, since I see you don't speak our language so easily? My French is not easy but I rather pride myself on my Latin, in spite of lack of practice."

This was, too, unexpected. "Latin by all means," said Blondel.

"Excellent. Here we are." He stood aside and motioned Blondel towards the entrance to a cave among the rocks; a little frightened, Blondel entered.

The ceiling of the cave was very high, as it should be, considering the proportions of its owner, but otherwise it was not particularly large. A place for a fire filled one end of it. A chair and a table, giant-size, furnished the other end of the cave. There was no other furniture except a broken chest near the fireplace. Blondel seated himself on a boulder near the fire and the giant lit a torch; then, busily, he lit the fire and, his household tasks done, he pulled his chair beside Blondel's rock.

"I would offer you this chair," he said politely, "but considering its size . . ." He gestured delicately to complete his meaning.

"I'm quite comfortable, said Blondel.

"So you're a troubadour. Well, under any other circumstances," again he gestured delicately with his great hand, "I

84

myself should have become a troubadour, too. As a child I was a choir boy and until I got my Growth everyone took it for granted I should become a troubadour. Well . . . life is so full of unfulfilled promise," he said and he sighed like a bellows. "But now you must sing me a song. One of those pleasant ballads you French do so well . . . about a merciless lady."

Blondel sang him one of these and the giant was very much moved. "Very touching," he said, clearing his throat. "Do you mind if I copy that down? It's one of your own, I presume?"

"Oh, yes." To his amazement the giant went to his table, took a pen and a piece of parchment. "Now would you say the words for me, please?" he asked, pen in hand; Blondel recited the ballad.

"You're surprised, perhaps, that I can write," said the giant, sitting down again in his chair near Blondel.

"Well . . . it is surprising," admitted Blondel, who had himself learned to write only with great difficulty. Some of the best troubadours could neither read nor write and relied on scribes to record their ballads.

"I was an unusually gifted child," said the giant comfortably, stretching his feet almost into the fire. "I was born in a small village outside Rome. I wasn't much different from other children in . . . in proportion but I was much quicker mentally, a natural scholar. When I was ten I struck the fancy of two Roman monks and they persuaded my family with, I regret to say, no difficulty to let them take me to their monastery to be educated. I was very happy in the monastery; I sang in the choir and one day a cardinal came and, after hearing me, said I had an excellent voice. Oh, I can remember that day as clearly as I remember yesterday. More clearly, I expect, since yesterday is so much like the days, the years I've already spent here . . . but to get on: I was taught to read and write, to copy manuscripts and even, at the immature age of twelve, I was allowed to illuminate certain documents . . . an unusual honor, as you must know, and one which I'm told my work merited." He cleared his throat, pausing in his stream of elegant Latin: few priests spoke as fluently and none with such style, thought Blondel, fascinated.

"For several years I lived happily in the monastery. The monks took it for granted that in time I would become one of them, but my heart was set on becoming a troubadour and I wrote songs secretly and sang them to myself; however, as all good things must, this period of my life, the sunlit period I like to consider it, came to an abrupt end when, quite suddenly, I obtained my Growth. The good monks regarded this as the devil's doing and after much consultation I was told to leave.

"You can imagine what I must have felt, a youth, a sensitive, even brilliant boy raised by holy men, unworldly and trusting, set loose on the world with an unusual stature. I went to Rome, where for a while I was engaged as a certain noble's troubadour; I ran away, however, when I learned that his guests paid no attention to my voice or songs, but were interested only in my height; they even laughed at me when I sang. It was too much to bear. I fled Rome, going northward. I won't bore you with the story of my travels. Enough to say that I suffered. I went from town to town, castle to castle; sometimes I remained awhile as a curiosity; more often I was driven into the fields, stoned in the streets. After years of this sort of life I came to Austria, found this cave and established myself here as a terrible monster; imagine! But at least they leave me alone now and I live quietly." He stopped and looked at the fire dreamily.

"A remarkable history," said Blondel sympathetically, "and a tragic one."

"Yes, it has an element of tragedy, I think. I keep busy, though. I write verse in Latin, in the manner of the ancients, who are, of course, the only great poets, the only models for a man of taste. We have no one today to compare with the dead Romans; no one at all . . . I wonder if you'd care to hear one of my own works? a pastoral?"

"Certainly," said Blondel. "I'd like to very much."

With a happy smile the giant took a pile of manuscripts from his table and put them on his lap. He picked up the first manuscript.

He read for over an hour and Blondel wondered if he could stand this reading another moment. The verse, though properly constructed, was the worst he'd ever heard: full of Christian sentiment and shepherd boys, all the pagan and Christian banalities mixed. Blondel, a little dazed, uncomfortable on his rock, sleepy, had finally given up all hope when the giant stopped. There was an embarrassed silence; then, tremulously, an author waiting judgment. "What do you think?"

"Brilliant," said Blondel in a tired voice which might have been, and certainly was, interpreted as the breathless voice of admiration.

"Oh, I'm so glad," said the giant, and he beamed. "You know, that's the only really unsatisfactory thing about my life now: no audience, no intelligent criticism; it's so seldom that a man of culture like yourself comes this way. Still, I suppose it's enough to do one's work; that's the real test of the poet: to work without an audience or a chance of fame like I've done, to work from a sense of dedication. And yet how satisfactory it must be to write for many people . . . well, each of us must follow his particular Muse and Destiny: mine is the way of the real poets, dedicated to saying what I must, indifferent to the lack of audience; yes, I think honestly indifferent when I work; I try only to please myself." He paused, his head posed as though he could see himself in a mirror.

"I think you're so right," said Blondel earnestly. "But still isn't it lonely here?" he asked, changing the subject, destroying the profile: the role of poet, for the time, discarded. "To live here year after year alone."

"It was at first, certainly, but now I enjoy the solitude. I write and I hunt. Then there are many shepherd boys in these hills; I like them."

"Of course," said Blondel. This last was somewhat alarming; he'd never before thought of a giant as a sexual creature and the thought of a giant with a taste for shepherd boys was disturbing. He himself was too old to be mistaken for a boy but still . . . he watched the giant nervously. This could be very serious. Only rather old nobles cared much for shepherd boys in France; at least that had been his experience. The giant continued to talk, however, unaware of his guest's alarm.

"But now," he was saying, "you must be hungry. Sit right there while I fix us something." The giant disappeared into the shadowy far end of the cave and Blondel measured with his eyes the distance to the door. If necessary he would run. If possible he'd like to eat first, however. The giant appeared again with a roast on a spit and a bottle of wine. He put the spit on and placed the bottle between them.

They chatted about the different troubadours, their various merits, and Blondel found his host surprisingly well informed. "As a medium I've always found the ballad difficult," remarked the giant. "Perhaps it's because of my rigidly classical background and technique. But of course it's a charming popular form, though not *precise* enough to satis-fy me. Ah, the roast's warm." He cut a slice for Blondel and one for himself; they ate without plates. Blondel was hungry and the food was good; he asked for more.

"You like this?" asked the giant, cutting him another piece smiling with pleasure, a pleased host and cook.

"Yes, very much."

"I'm so glad. He was a good-looking boy, about sixteen I'd guess; much the best age. I was afraid he'd be too muscular but he's really quite tender. He had an excellent natural singing voice, untrained, of course, but he knew a number of village songs I'd never heard before. I took them down and if you like I'll sing them to you later . . . what on earth's the matter? I thought you said you liked it?" Blondel was sick.

"Oh, I'm so sorry; I should have told you first and given you some mutton or something instead. Do forgive me. Here, wait a moment . . ." The giant moved quickly but Blondel was faster. He ran out of the cave, dodging from rock to rock in the darkness. He could hear, echoing in the gorge, the giant's voice, pleading, "Come back; please come back."

But Blondel ran until he felt safe and, panting, his heart racing, he fell on his face and was sick again.

That night he sat in a tree, unable to sleep, unable to for-get what had happened. Stars shone against the black, making no shadows and little light. He waited for the sun to rise.

4

Snow was falling in Vienna. The flakes were large and soft and took a long time to melt; one rested on his eyelashes for a minute before it became a trickle of water. The snow massed deep and soft on the streets, covering the cobbles, hiding refuse: streets of white marble. Snow gathered on the steep roofs; snow hid the towers and spires of churches and palaces, obscuring the outlines of even the nearest buildings. There was almost no sound in the city even though people walked in the streets and horsemen rode, the sound of their horses' hoofs deadened in the whiteness. The morning seemed like evening, sunless, still and gray, and the voices of people were low, muffled by whiteness.

Blondel was tired and his legs had begun to ache; fortunately the day was not cold. The muscles of his thighs were knotted from too much walking. He paused a moment in the street and rested. He had already decided that he would present himself at the Duke's palace as a troubadour; if Richard was there he would find him; if not he would find out very soon where he was: there were no secrets at a court. After that . . . after that he would travel again.

He moved down the street and, at the sign of the first cookshop, went in and ate a large meal. The men who sat with him at table, tradesmen mostly, discussed the gossip of the town and the day. The Emperor, it seemed, had just arrived at the ducal court. There were rumors that Leopold had seized the Pope, captured Saladin, murdered Philip of France, imprisoned Richard of England; no one knew exactly what had happened but everyone had an opinion and no one reserved it.

Then, having learned nothing but the public fact that the Emperor was in Vienna, Blondel went to a shop where tunics were sold and bought himself a dark green one which, as he had learned long ago, would set off the color of his eyes. He had a little gold and much silver left from Tiernstein: enough to live on for a while but not enough to buy a horse. He washed himself in a bowl the tunic-maker provided; then he pulled the tunic over his head and looked at himself in a small mirror. He was thinner and harder than he had been before the landing at Zara. His face was brown from wind and cold and new lines had appeared about his eyes, but his back had healed at last and he was, finally, comfortable. The tunic-maker directed him to the ducal palace.

"I am a troubadour," he announced ceremoniously, "Raimond of Perpignan." There would be people in Vienna who had heard of Raimond of Toulouse; he would be an imaginary troubadour now. "I have just arrived from Palestine on my way to Paris. I heard in the city that the Duke was receiving the Emperor and I thought I would like to sing for them, if that's not too much of a request; it would be a great honor." The guard let him pass. He was received in a small, high-ceilinged, draughty room by a thin man in black who was introduced as one of the chamberlains.

"Raimond of Perpignan? Philip is your King?"

"Philip, of course, Excellency."

"Where have you sung before? what courts?"

"Marseilles, Blois, at the King's in Paris."

"You were with Philip in Palestine?"

"Yes."

"Why didn't you return when he did? He is already in Paris."

"I was ill for some time at Ascalon. I'm traveling slowly now across Europe, visiting different courts."

"Where have you sung in Austria?"

"Most recently at Tiernstein."

The Chamberlain nodded. "The Lord and Lady of Tiernstein will arrive here in a week or so." Blondel decided he would be gone before that. "Now sing for me." And Blondel sang a short ballad and the Chamberlain nodded, pleased. "An excellent voice, Master Raimond, and the song is good, too. You may join the other troubadours tonight. There will be a contest I think and the Duke, who has a fine voice and a great talent for improvisation, may sing, too. You improvise, of course?"

"Of course; but only in French."

"All the singing, I believe, will be in French. The others are mostly French. Now, since you'll be singing before the Emperor, there're certain ceremonies which you must know." And the Chamberlain explained to him how he should act when he was presented. He was then shown a room which he would share with two other troubadours. After this he was left alone; the contest wouldn't begin until late that night when the banquet in the great hall was over.

He walked about the palace, down long corridors among servants and guardsmen laughing and talking and doing errands. Finally he came to a long room decorated with tapestries and highly carved benches. A carved table ran beneath the several deep-set windows. Courtiers, men and women both, at least a hundred of them, chattered together, occasionally wandering, in pairs down an adjacent gallery, arranging intrigues, no doubt, and doing the business of the country. This was the Austrian court. The women were stouter than Frenchwomen and not so tall as the Saxon ones; most of them were fair and a few had red hair; Blondel particularly liked red-haired women: there were so few in the part of France where he'd spent most of his life. The voices of the Austrian women were high and they laughed a great deal, shrieking like those vivid birds explorers sometimes brought back from Africa. Their headdresses were often elaborate, bejeweled, and their veils were of silk and finely made. He was ignored in the confusion and he passed among them invisibly, an audience to their unconscious performance. The men were, if young, sturdy and slim, but almost all of the ones older than thirty were fat and red-faced, not unlike the Lord of Tiernstein. They talked animatedly and seemed genuinely well disposed towards one another, unlike the courtiers of other countries. Some spoke German; many spoke Latin and some talked in French with strong accents. At intervals one of the tall doors at the end of the room opposite the gallery would open and a chamberlain would call out the name of some courtier who would be granted an audience with the Emperor.

Listening to conversations, Blondel learned that the Emperor would remain in Vienna several weeks, that he was having some quarrel with the Duke, that the cause of the quarrel was a secret shared by all of them; they smiled at one another, winked, and remarked that their Duke was in a difficult position.

Finally, tired of listening to the talk and more tired of standing, Blondel sat down on one of the benches. He had never felt so unreal, so isolated, in his life. He wanted suddenly to be back in France, to be sixteen again, to have his mother living and to work in the fields every day under the warm sun. He remembered the priest who had taught him to read; he remembered the baron in the nearby castle who had had him sing for him when he was only seventeen and his head was full of words and music, waiting for direction, and the direction came when he sang for people and they listened to him and applauded. Then he had moved from court to court, across France, into England, once to Italy and, finally, the crusade with Richard. Now, after many years, he wanted to go back, to be in one place with one person. Someone who would be even more than a friend, someone protective; perhaps Richard or perhaps a woman like Amelia: someone wiser than he and kind. But now he was lost, without a center, quite alone, and he was terrified. He hadn't felt this way since he was a boy. For an instant he saw the entire world as menacing and, worst of all, impersonal in its cruelty. He was part of continual change: he would age and his body would become weak and his face loose, grotesque. His voice would go and then what would he do? where would he go to live the last years of his life, the years of ugliness? If anything happened to Richard he would be lost, without protection; his other friends, several lords, were not close enough to him, gave him no sense of security, no protection from the menace. He was cold now; he shivered; his hands were sweaty. And all around him, laughing and talking, were the stout men and the sturdy women of the court of Austria, each with a castle of stone, many relatives and noble ancestors, much land and gold. They would live a long time, most of them; they would be honored and respected in their own castles and their wealth would protect them from this terror, while he was only a traveler, a troubadour with no castle to retreat to; all he had in the world was the friendship of a prisoner King. He thought of Richard to comfort himself, recalled his harsh voice, heard it in his mind, sounding above the noise of courtiers babbling; his future was there, his direction clear to find the King and help set him free. He must remember this, must never allow it out of his mind. It was so easy to forget when one was alone among strangers in an unfamiliar and hostile city; but he would remember now. He made a picture in his mind: the face smiling and the blue eyes watchful; he saw him standing waist-deep in the black pond of the forest. He heard his voice shouting as he charged the Saracens at Acre. When he thought of Richard he thought of movement, a powerful arm, with knotted muscles, striking with a sword. The present was only a hiatus, a space to be got through quickly; and, dreaming of the King, he forgot his loneliness and remembered what he must do, recognizing the center towards which he must move.

Blondel sat at one of the smaller tables with the other troubadours. He had heard of only one of them, a large conceited fellow from Orleans who, not finding much favor in the courts of France, had for years sung in Austria and the provincial cities of central Europe. The other troubadours were either very young and still unknown or else older men, past fifty, whose reputations had vanished years before when the old courts of their youth had changed, when their first protectors, their first mistresses had died or grown too old to care for them, to be concerned with remembering. Blondel was always polite to the old troubadours and they were grateful.

Fortunately most of them were strangers to one another. All knew, by reputation, of the man from Orleans. He sat at the head of their table and spoke very solemnly and a little disparagingly of Vidal, of Blondel, of Hautefort, of Born, of Raimond of Vaquerias, in fact of all the distinguished troubadours. "And what, Sir," asked Blondel with elaborate courtesy, "do you think of Blondel? Why do you find his singing bad?"

The man from Orleans cleared his throat and fingered his dark beard with a plump hairy hand. "A good technician," he said slowly. "I've heard him sing many times, of course. I found his voice a bit weak and he has very little range. Quite a minor troubadour really. If it hadn't been for Richard, I'm sure he'd never have become known. An excellent courtier, of course. Perhaps a better courtier than a troubadour, but that's the sure way to success: to be friendly with kings. It isn't necessary to have talent if one is."

"What sort of man is Blondel?" asked Blondel, enjoying this.

The man shrugged. "Middle-aged, I should say. Rather heavy stature and quite superficial as a person. I don't really believe he feels what he sings and composes. Some think he has great personal charm but I've never noticed it. But of course he must have some charm or Richard would never had taken such a fancy to him. But then Richard is very susceptible to flattery (as we all know) and Blondel is excellent at that.

"I believe," said the man from Orleans thoughtfully, "that the greatest satisfaction is to compose just as one pleases without trying to please a particular patron. Many of the best-known troubadours try too hard to please a patron and that's why their work won't last." He paused and the younger troubadours leaned forward to learn. "I have always composed and sung to please people, and myself. I haven't resorted to the technical tricks of Blondel or the fashionable 'rough' diction of Vidal to attract attention; no, I work in the broad, the popular tradition; but still my own manner, of course." The young men nodded as though they had learned a good deal; the older troubadours were too busy eating to listen to this. Blondel, however, was fascinated and he wondered if the Orleans man had actually ever seen him before; probably not, from his description. He was a familiar type and in the German courts had found, no doubt, the success he could never have had in France. With a few more irritable words about his contemporaries, the man from Orleans filled his mouth with food and Blondel, himself eating, looked about the great hall, appreciating the magnificence and the comparative cleanliness.

There were many long carved tables, heavy with food and gold and silver plate. Servants hurried in and out; dogs snuffed about, looking for bones and scraps. The hall was divided into three parts, each opening into the next through a high arch of stone and wood. Doors opened out of all four walls of the hall and, on the second floor, an open gallery overlooked the diners. Huge wooden beams held up the ceiling, and tapestries and standards, bright and many-colored, some smoke-darkened, hung from the walls: trophies of forgotten wars and Austrian victories. The hall was full of color and sound and the smell of roasting meat. A loud noise of talk made it impossible to be heard without shouting. At the opposite end of the hall Blondel could see a small table on a dais, and here, he knew, sat the Holy Roman Emperor and the Duke. He recognized Leopold; and a short plump man with light hair, slightly receding chin and a white face, dressed in scarlet and wearing several gold chains about his neck, was, or so the man beside him said, the Emperor Henry. Blondel was too far away to make out the details of his face.

Brilliantly dressed nobles sat at the tables nearest the dais and then at the tables nearest Blondel's own, knights, monks and men-at-arms sat, the noisiest of all. Everyone drank a great deal and acted childishly. One knight emptied a plate on another's head and everyone laughed as the knight threw a flagon of wine as reprisal, splattering the table with purple. Very different, thought Blondel critically, from the courts of France.

After what seemed many hours of heavy eating, the Chamberlain got to his feet in front of the dais and, with a wand of office, struck one of the tables a loud blow. The voices dropped to a murmur. The Chamberlain announced that among other entertainment, there would be a contest of troubadours. The Emperor and the ladies of the Imperial family, several fat youngish women Blondel had already

97

noticed, would be judges. The Duke Leopold, the Chamberlain continued, would take part in the contest. Everyone cheered at this and the Duke nodded and smiled. Blondel loathed him.

The troubadours, eleven of them not counting the Duke, came forward. As they were presented Blondel examined the Emperor curiously. He was young, only twenty-seven, but sickness had made him look older; there were dark shadows under his eyes and one eyelid twitched nervously. Blondel found it hard to believe that this was, in theory, the descendant of the Caesars. Henry was a small man, unlike his red-bearded father who had once walked barefoot for the Pope. His face was tallow-pale, sickly, with small features. His eyes were heavy-lidded and he seemed almost asleep, his face expressionless. He murmured a few words to the troubadours which no one heard; then he rested his head in two surprisingly large, strong, beringed and dirty-fingered hands. Quickly Blondel looked at the ladies of the Imperial family: one was rather pretty, reddish-haired and young. He looked at her directly and she, having already noticed him, looked back, turned pink and looked away. Now he would sing to her. He smiled and knew that she had seen his smile, for she quickly took a bone from her plate and gnawed at it delicately with a preoccupied expression. At least he had one ally, one favorable decision. They were then instructed in their order: the man from Orleans first; Blondel next to last and the Duke Leopold the last. The Duke, of course, would win, but perhaps he himself would do well enough to receive a present.

Then the Imperial family went into a serious conference, whispering to one another; even the Emperor seemed interested and he listened to his women, nodding from time to time. At last they were agreed: the two opening verses had been selected. The Emperor said them to the Chamberlain, who announced them to the troubadours and the assembly. "The opening verses set of the improvisations will be: 'My heart set me going, when I should have been ceasing.' The troubadour from Orleans will begin."

Blondel wished the lines were better; he wondered if his particular Lady had selected them. He glanced at her but she was busy with her bone. The Holy Roman Emperor again supported his head on his hands, his eyes almost closed as though in contemplation of empire and of decline. Everyone else waited eagerly for the man from Orleans to begin. The other troubadours were nervous, tuning their viols, talking to themselves, muttering phrases and rhymes, clearing their throats and humming. Leopold sat among them, prepared, smiling confidently. Blondel was quite sure he had been told the lines in advance and his ballad was already made. Well, he wouldn't think of that. He would have to improvise something extraordinary. He decided: he would do a trick that had been seldom done in France and probably never in Austria. He would sing a duet with the Song he sang: it would be like a dialogue between himself and his own Song, each addressing the other. The tone would be respectful but a bit ironic. The others, he was quite sure, would be serious and sentimental; he was sure of all of them except Leopold.

The man from Orleans began. His voice was loud, deep and not quite true. He was aware of this and he tried to disguise his faults by large gestures and increased volume. He sang a serious love ballad which, Blondel was confident, he had sung many times before, changing only a phrase here and there to fit it with the first two lines. One by one the others sang. A few of the young men had good voices and a few of the older ones were facile and clever in composing; but he knew he was the only real troubadour among them and, by rights, he should win the prize.

"Raimond of Perpignan," announced the Chamberlain, and Blondel stood up and walked to the open place before the dais. He bowed deeply to the Emperor, who did not look at him but contemplated a design of Saracen shields on the near wall. He bowed to the ladies and they nodded; his ally smiled shyly.

He turned to the audience, struck some notes on his viol and then announced in a ringing voice the first two lines of the ballad. The murmur of voices stopped and everyone watched him. For the first time the Emperor looked at him, conscious of authority. Now he would show them. He began in a low voice.

He glanced at the Imperial family and saw that their eyes were on him and the mouth of his ally was slightly open.

He looked at the Duke and saw that he was frowning slightly, his fingers scratching the table.

Then he sang the conversation between himself and the Song.

The audience at first didn't realize what he was doing. As they came to understand, they smiled and began to cheer. The Chamberlain quieted them and, triumphantly, Blondel sang the *envoi*.

There was great applause when he finished. He bowed again to the Emperor, who congratulated him, almost audibly, in Latin. His ally threw him a ribbon of pale silk which he took and kissed, to the pleasure of the audience. Then he went back to his seat, the sound of shouting still in his ears.

It was now Leopold's turn. He looked unpleasantly at Blondel as he walked towards the dais, smiled at Henry and his family, and bowed when they nodded, although their eyes were still on Blondel, who sat beside the man from

Orleans, modestly examining the viol in his lap. Blondel wondered if perhaps any of them suspected him: the mannerisms of famous troubadours were well known; fortunately, though, he hadn't sung a typical Blondel ballad.

Leopold sang well. His voice was light without much range but it was true and the ballad he sang, though ordinary and sentimental, was elegant in construction and in the best modern tradition. Blondel was certain it had been composed in advance; he wondered by whom.

Leopold was much applauded when he finished. His courtiers outdid one another in cheering. The Imperial family also applauded but a bit perfunctorily, thought Blondel, who after many years could interpret exactly an audience's response.

Then the Emperor and his ladies went into a serious conference. Several times they looked at Blondel and he knew that he might still win the contest and the bag of gold which stood on a stool beside the dais. At last, after what appeared to be disagreement, the Emperor said the name of the victor and the Chamberlain with a great smile announced: "The winner of this contest is our gracious Duke, Leopold!"

More applause from the courtiers. Leopold stood up and bowed. He was serene, smiling again, his full lips as soft and as red as a girl's. Then, when there was quiet, he said, "As a reward for an excellent song I shall give the gold to the troubadour, Raimond of Perpignan." And he walked over to Blondel and gave him the prize. There was even more applause after this and Blondel saw that everyone was pleased: he had had no idea the Duke was so clever, for now they were all exclaiming at his generosity. The Emperor took one of his many gold chains and tossed it to Blondel, who caught it, bowing. Then jugglers appeared and the troubadours withdrew to their end of the hall.

"A good performance," said the man from Orleans heavily. "I've never heard that trick done before but you sang it well, considering. You must have appeared a great deal in the courts of France."

"Only in Provence," he said; he would be wary. "And once in Paris."

"You have the fashionable manner," said the other, trying to be pleasant. "Of course, as you know, fashions change so quickly; I've always felt that those who follow contemporary fashions must accept the fact that they'll be unfashionable themselves one day."

"You're absolutely right," said Blondel humbly.

"Myself, I've never been influenced by the new schools that one hears about all the time. The ballad is essentially a pure, a set classic form, and I see no reason to vary it because of some singer's desire to make an unusual effect; *I* think it's an admission that he can't work in the conventional forms, that's what I think."

"That's so true."

The other man looked at him suspiciously, not prepared for such humility. "I'm sure you'd be very popular at the French courts. They like your sort of inventiveness. I hear that Richard is also a devotee of the *strange*. I should hate to feel that a beautiful form like the traditional ballad could become so inadequate that I'd feel *I* had to change it, make it into something else."

"One does it only for effect."

"I agree certainly. But is the effect of the moment worth damaging one's integrity, the integrity of the medium?"

"I can't see it does much harm," said Blondel and, purposely, he sounded cynical, convincing the other he was only a trickster of no account; he succeeded.

"Well, of course, I can see how many people are tempted

to be dishonest; that's not uncommon," and the man from Orleans spoke no more to Blondel.

The younger troubadours, however, gathered around Blondel admiringly and asked him technical questions; they were all surprised he was not a more famous troubadour. At last, when the entertainment was over, the courtiers and the knights wandered about the great hall, still drinking, talking and intriguing. The Duke and the Imperial party had disappeared.

Blondel wandered from group to group, accepting congratulations, listening. He joined occasional groups and waited to hear what they might say of Richard but no one mentioned him and he dared not ask. He knew that it was more than likely someone here had heard him sing in Palestine, had recognized him and would report him to the Duke. He would have to leave tonight; but now, for a time, he must stay, inconspicuous and listening.

Suddenly he recalled what Otto had told him about his friend at court, Stefan of Dreisen. He asked several people if they knew him, and finally a drunken knight pointed with a sausage finger to a dark slim man standing a few feet away.

"Stefan of Dreisen?"

"Yes?" the dark young man turned and looked at Blondel; he was good-looking in a boyish sulky way.

"I was told to see you if I came to Vienna. Your friend Otto at Tiernstein told me to see you."

The young man smiled. "Oh, you saw Otto; yes, he's my closest friend. How was he when you left him?"

"Well, I thought restless, perhaps."

"Poor Otto. I don't see how he stands Tiernstein. You met the Lady Hedwig, of course?"

Blondel grimaced and Stefan laughed. "I escaped that fate by running from her apartment so fast that even if she did yell I'd be so far away she would look silly saying I'd attacked her. What did you do?"

Blondel told him and Stefan laughed and asked, when he'd finished, "Now tell me; is Otto coming to Vienna or not? I've heard the Lord and Lady are, but no word about him."

Blondel said he didn't know, that it was some time since he'd been at Tiernstein. Then Stefan took his arm and they found a bench beneath the gallery and here they sat and talked, ignoring the crowds of drunken men about them. They drank and talked of everything, of armies and troubadours, of the intrigues of kings, of giants and dragons, of Saracens and hell. Blondel enjoyed Stefan. He had charm and much wit. He had no respect for his superiors; a good sign, Blondel had always found. He told irreverent anecdotes about Leopold, about his ambitions to become, at least, a king, of his trouble with the Emperor now.

"The trouble is over Richard, isn't it?" asked Blondel.

Stefan nodded. "I suppose you know, too; like everybody else in Vienna. Only I don't think the English know yet; at least not where he is or what's to be done with him. There are rumors that Philip is sending us a special ambassador, and heaven knows what sort of trouble we're going to get into with the Pope."

"But what are Leopold and the Emperor quarreling about?"

"Over Richard, of course. The Emperor wants him and I expect he'll just take him no matter what Leopold says. Then there'll be real trouble. They are trying to agree on the ransom now, on the division of it. Leopold has a great many debts; most of them inherited, and he has to pay them off before he can go kingdom-building. Henry, on the other hand, is just naturally greedy . . . I should like to listen to those two sometime: Leopold smiling and smiling and

Henry looking sicker and sicker. Well, the Emperor will get Richard all right but Leopold will be difficult."

"Where is he now?"

"Oh, I expect they're in the Emperor's apartments talking."

"No, I meant Richard . . . where's he?"

"At Lintz, in the castle there. They say he's been a real terror. He has everyone frightened of him. He holds court with his guards and he fights them, wins their money at dice and eats enormous amounts. They say he goes into rages and threatens the lord of the castle, swears at him and tries to shake the walls down. He must be a wonderful man from all accounts. I think it was silly of Leopold to seize him considering on what good terms he was with the Pope. There might even be a war if we're not careful. Depends a lot on what Philip's embassy has to say, of course."

"Then they don't keep him in a dungeon."

"Lion-Heart! the pride of Christendom! Not even Leopold would be that stupid. No, he's just a guest who can't leave. By the way, I hear he's been writing ballads."

"I'm not surprised," said Blondel. "We sing some of his ballads in France. They're quite good."

"If he writes them himself. I hear his troubadour friend, Blondel, writes them for him."

Blondel grew cold an instant. "I've heard that, too."

"I live in the city," said Stefan. "You could spend the night here with me. It would be much more comfortable than the palace, less noise."

"I'd like to," said Blondel, who was eager to leave this place before he was recognized.

They made their way through the crowded hall. The heat was terrible from the fire, from torches and many bodies; it was difficult to breathe. They stepped over drunken men, asleep on the floor. Such things never happened at great courts, thought Blondel fastidiously.

"I'll have to leave early in the morning," said Blondel, avoiding two quarreling men who had drawn their swords.

"As soon as that?"

5

Early the next morning he left Vienna. During the night a hard crust had formed on the snow. The day began, dazzling with winter light reflected on the snow: red, yellow and violet lights glittered in the whiteness. The sky was a deep winter-blue, and in the sun he was warm. He loosed his cloak, cool air touched him and, behind the coolness, the sun burned. People walked in the streets; they looked cheerful, reflecting the weather of the day as people will. Carts rattled, and groups of mounted men-at-arms rode in the snow-smoothed streets towards the frontiers of Austria, towards rebellions and unknown battles.

He rode again, on a horse bought with the Emperor's prize; he was pleased with his own success the night before and with the money, for the gold would last him until he got to Richard, at least. He hummed happily as he rode on to the highway to Lintz.

Rolling country, white and shining, swept away from the city, up from the broad river; fields like patches of white and clumps of trees like black and twisted old men's fingers scratching light. He had the highway to himself and he rode, breathing the air consciously, with pleasure, a part of motion, aware of sharpness and a sudden clarity. No clouds in the sky: all of it blue, clear and startlingly, eye-wateringly vivid, the color of sapphires or a king's eyes. No wind disturbed the air as he rode through whiteness.

Days passed.

Towards some further mystery time moved, and the days, the moments of light and dark passed and he moved, like time, towards a mystery he could not name, a place beyond illusion, larger than the moment, enlarged by death. He had no idea of the future; vaguely he realized he must move towards Richard but beyond that he did not think, and at times even Richard seemed barely to exist for him. He moved and that was all. He went through villages and saw the peasants working. He heard them talk to one another and he knew that each of them had a history known to the others while, among them, he alone was different, without a history or a reality in these villages: no recognition ever, only curiosity, a fair-skinned man, still young, who paid for a place to sleep and for food.

He was the stranger.

The children were the most suspicious and the most interested; they would stand in groups near him, pointing and watching, afraid of him. For a long time he had smiled at the children but then he found this frightened them and so, finally, he learned to look at people without expression, as though they had no existence for him, as though they too were ghosts. And actually he differed from them only in the fact of motion: they seldom moved beyond their villages, for they feared giants and dragons, werewolves and vampires and, above all, other men. But the people who have no future and no history can go from place to place fearing nothing since they are protected by the present; they recognize none of the boundaries of time; they cross no frontiers: they move only in the present across the world, and only a few, like Blondel, realize, if only vaguely, that they must find a king; although the search itself is enough reason to forget one's history, sufficient cause to destroy the fact of the future, which is at best an abstraction and a dream.

The traveler, the stranger, the separate man: moving from nowhere to nowhere, pondering at certain times a captured king: this was Blondel who crossed the winter-frozen, snow-streaked hills of Austria and shivered, as all travelers do, when the wind was cold.

"So, just back from Palestine? I was there; I was at Acre."

Everyone, thought Blondel, every knight in Europe had been at Acre! "I was there, too," said Blondel.

"Oh, is that so? I don't guess any of us will ever forget those days. We'll be telling our grandchildren about them, I expect. I know I'll never forget the night before the final battle; I rode with Duke Leopold through our camp and he talked to the men and told them they were in the middle of the greatest, the most important war in the history of the world. Imagine that!"

Blondel said that he could imagine that. The young knight poured himself more wine. He was tall and heavily built, with strong hairy arms. His hair was black and his cheekbones high; he looked as if he might have had some oriental blood. His eyebrows grew together, a line of black fur giving his face a sinister look.

"Whose army were you with at Acre?" he asked and he took a long swallow of wine; Blondel could hear it gurgling in his throat and stomach.

"Philip Augustus'; I was one of his troubadours."

"A troubadour? That's pretty good. Always thought I might like to be one myself. I've a pretty good voice, you know, but I can't remember songs so well and I'm sure I couldn't write any. I tried making up one for *my* lady, the one I'm going to marry, I think; but I didn't get very far.

We're going to be married next month or as soon as her father decides. They live not far from Lintz; I'm going there now. He wants her to marry some really important lord but she wants to marry me and, since there isn't any important lord in sight, she can do a lot worse than me." He flexed the muscles of his arms complacently. "But weren't we talking about Acre? We fought the most the next day and the French didn't do much, if you'll excuse me saying so."

"What about Richard's army?"

The young man scowled. "He did almost as little as the French but he made more noise, shouting and carrying on. Then, after we'd taken most of the fortifications, he marched in and took over, just because he was a king."

"He struck your standards, too, as I remember."

He nodded. No, not even the eyebrows could make him look really sinister; or even intelligent, thought Blondel. "There wasn't much we could do once that devil took over. He had more men than we had, you know. Our Duke didn't bother to protest; it was too late. Everyone knows how greedy Richard is. I can forgive that, I guess, but it's the stories he has people spread about his bravery: that's what really is bad. He has a group of troubadours who do nothing but sing about him and call him Lion-Heart when actually he's like any general: he takes good care of himself."

"I always heard," said Blondel slowly, studying the scarred wood table in front of him, "that he really was brave."

"Brave! You heard the way he murdered Conrad of Montferrat, didn't you? I don't think there was anything brave about that. You want some more wine?"

Blondel took some more wine. It had grown late and they were the only people awake in the inn. Firelight reddened the smoke-dark walls of the room. Two travelers slept on the floor in front of the fire.

109

Blondel had met the young knight in the streets of Lintz and the latter had suggested they stay at the inn instead of the castle, which, he had heard, was full of visitors engaged in some intrigue: earlier, he had tried to see the lord of the castle and, though an acquaintance, he hadn't been able to get past the guards.

The next morning Blondel and his friend discovered why they had been barred from the castle. It was full of the Emperor's soldiers, who had been there for a week and, in spite of Duke Leopold, had seized Richard and one night (exactly when no one knew) had taken him off to the Emperor's castle at Durenstein.

Blondel learned all of this that morning, from soldiers of the Duke and from a monk who had been in the castle and who had actually seen Richard: "a large man with a violent temper; he laughed when the Emperor's men came to take him out of Austria."

Blondel was suddenly weary and, for the first time, discouraged. He would have to go many miles again to yet another castle, across more boundaries, enduring more cold days, and then, very likely, he would arrive only to find that they had moved the King again and he would have to travel still farther on his endless journey.

In Lintz Blondel inquired discreetly where Durenstein might be and then, more or less sure of the direction, he rode with the young knight out of Lintz.

For a time they discussed different weapons; then they discussed strains of horses; then they talked of Acre and, then, the young man's conversation exhausted, they discussed, all over again, preferences in weapons and, since no new ideas had occurred to either of them, they rode, at last, in silence through the forest.

The trees were taller than the ones around Vienna and

wind sounded in the higher branches, clattered and sighed, wood striking wood and twigs crackling and, above all, a strange sigh like the noise the dying sometimes make. Yet it was pleasant, he thought, to ride with someone again: to hear another man, another human being moving and breathing beside one, to strike occasionally, with a clanging sound, the metal of another's stirrups. Strange not really to mind loneliness when he traveled and yet want at the same time to have someone near him, even a dull young knight who knew about weapons, horses, the battle at Acre, and, unfortunately, nothing more.

They had tried to talk politics and the young man had said that he admired Leopold, respected the Emperor, revered the Pope, worshiped his lady's father, mistrusted Philip Augustus, despised Richard and hated Saladin, who was the devil on earth or, if not the devil himself, had at least been instructed by that dark prince to slaughter young knights from Austria and, if possible, to steal their souls. How this last was done he wasn't quite sure, but obviously there must be a way, for if not, why would the devil act through Saladin? Yes, that was logical, Blondel agreed.

"But she's so wonderful!" And here the young knight was at last articulate. "Her eyes are gray, you know; the color of those swords you buy in Palestine, that color. Her hair is dark but not as dark as mine and I think it's got some red in it; but it's her smile that's so wonderful. She has some sort of dimple, in her chin of all places; don't you think that's extraordinary? I do. That was the first thing I ever noticed about her. She's eighteen now; just the proper age to marry. I'm twenty so we're pretty much the same except for my experience, and that's the way it should be. I've never liked the idea of old men marrying young girls.

"She's very intelligent, too, for a woman, and she doesn't

talk much, thank God! I hate them when they talk all the time and that's just what they do in Vienna. You've been to court, haven't you? Well, they're really terrible; almost as bad as French women are supposed to be, if you'll excuse me. I don't think women should talk much because usually they don't know very much."

Blondel, hearing this last, nodded and smiled and thought the same applied to young knights.

Sometimes he listened to the boy but, more often, he let the harsh, still adolescent voice ramble on: a background for his own thoughts. Occasionally he would listen to a word here and there but more often not; it pleased the boy to talk and that was enough. Blondel found that he himself had got out of the habit of talking, and then, German was still difficult for him.

So they rode, side by side, harnesses creaking, stirrups clashing from time to time and the voice of the knight reciting endless stories about himself.

Their first night together in the forest, they made a fire by a spring. Shortly after midnight they were attacked by werewolves. The young knight's shouts awakened Blondel; three men in gray wolf-skin tunics held them to the ground and two more were ready to do the same to Blondel. Quickly he got to his feet and, before they could seize him, he pulled out the silver pentagram and showed it to them. The two men stopped and stared at the medallion.

"Where'd you get this?" asked one, a dreadful-looking man with a withered ear.

"From Stefan near Tiernstein," said Blondel quickly.

"You know him?"

"Yes. I'm a troubadour; I sang for him."

"Stefan likes music," said one of the men as though in explanation.

The man with the withered ear looked irritated. "Of course, we must respect the sign," he said, "but I think you should give us a present: one fourth of all you have, say."

The young knight on the ground began to roar: he would fight any two of them if they'd let him up; he'd teach them a lesson . . . one of the men kicked him and he stopped talking.

"Certainly," Blondel agreed, "but you'll have to give us safe passage through your forest; we don't want more of your people asking for presents; we're poor men ourselves."

"You won't be bothered," said the thief, and carefully he counted out one fourth of the knight's gold and then, as scrupulously, one fourth of Blondel's.

At last, this delicate problem settled, he waved and said, "You won't be bothered again tonight and by tomorrow afternoon you'll be out of the forest." The men disappeared so quickly that, for a moment, Blondel wondered (as he had wondered once before) if after all there might not really be magic creatures in the world who could be wolves when they chose or who could vanish, become air if they chose.

"We should have fought them. You shouldn't have given the gold away without fighting. I'd sooner have died than let those thieves rob me like that." The young knight rubbed the place where he had been kicked.

"I didn't think there was much else we could do," said Blondel irritably. "They were sitting on top of you and I wasn't armed; besides I think we're lucky to get off so easily."

"I'd like to meet the one-eared devil again. I'd teach him . . ." For about an hour the young knight spoke of what he would do if he ever saw the one-eared man again. Wolves howled. After a time they slept.

Blondel was invited to stay at Wenschloss, the castle of his companion's lady. The invitation was offered him only after he had given a long and detailed account of how he happened to be wearing the silver medallion of the werewolves.

Wenschloss was a bleak little castle set on a bare slate-dark rock overlooking a gorge where a river crashed between narrow stone banks, upon boulders; a ribbon of water twisted by the stone.

The castle's keep was of solid masonry but most of the buildings and parts of the protecting walls were wood. There was a village at the base of the rock where the castle stood; cultivated fields extended between the river and the forest's edge. Just north of the castle was a wooden bridge, and beyond it a road which led, he was told, towards Durenstein.

The family of Wenschloss had, as sometimes happens, assumed the characteristics of their own estates. They were dark like their forests, with jaws heavy and squared like the rocks of the river; their eyes were as gray, as clear and as cold as the river's water. They received Blondel politely and they listened to the young knight's description of the werewolf attack. The family of Wenschloss spoke seldom and even Blondel's friend, soon to be their relative, stopped talking finally. They inquired about the general political situation; beyond that they were not concerned with the life in Vienna or even at Lintz.

When supper was finished in the hall, a gloomy, draughty place with ridiculously few torches considering the vast forests the Wenschlosses owned, they all sat in throne-like chairs about the fire and no one spoke. To Blondel's great surprise, no one asked him to sing. They sat and studied the fire and, occasionally, one another; even Blondel's companion was affected, was silent, looking mostly at his bride-to-be.

She was a pretty girl, too plump for Blondel's taste, with the sort of body which, in a few years, would be absolutely round. Germans rather liked that sort of thing, though. It was strange how tastes varied from country to country. All a matter of habit, really, of what one was used to. She seemed a nice girl and she obviously adored her knight, for she looked at him solemnly with great eyes, rather like a fascinated chipmunk, her small round hands folded helplessly in her lap. Blondel tried to imagine them together.

Her father was a warrior-patriarch; his hair and beard like tree bark and his face like clumsily carved wood. He almost never spoke.

They sat looking at one another for an hour. Finally, when the fire went out and smoke filled the hall and made them weep, the family of Wenschloss, without a word, rose and withdrew. Servants led Blondel and the young knight to their rooms.

He slept well that night. The next morning, while the sky was still gathering light, he ordered his horse from the groom and, imitating the manners of his hosts, departed without a word.

He crossed the river and entered another forest; here the trees were twisted and gnarled as though they had been attacked by some terrible wind.

A day, a night passed and he had adjusted himself to traveling alone again. Every night a strong wind blew in the forest, a black wind which blotted out the stars like a heavy cloak held between the trees and the sky. He spent several such nights in this forest and each night this bitter wind blew and the stars vanished.

No wolves called in the forest: no sound at all; he wondered if this was an enchanted forest, like the dragon's forest.

There were times when he believed in magic. Spells and incantations he regarded sceptically; they were, of course, only used to frighten the ignorant. But the larger enchantments: the transformations of entire cities, the blighting of forests, the cursing of mountains – he could accept such things and he had been told of witches who could make lightning and storms. All this was possible. Then, as for giants and dragons, he had seen these creatures himself. His giant hadn't really been very tall, at least not as tall as giants were usually said to be, but he had been quite unusual. The dragon was the most unusual of all: Blondel had never seen another animal like it, but even so, the dragon hadn't been like the legendary fire-breathing monsters he had heard of. The werewolves were, in one sense, the greatest disappointment. All his life he had heard village stories about men who, when the moon came full, turned into wolves and hunted for a night with the wolf pack, becoming, the next day, men again, with blood on their clothes and no memory. Perhaps, somewhere, there were really such creatures as werewolves though it seemed unlikely now: merely bands of thieves hiding in the forests of Europe, loosely united by the symbols of the wolf and their common banditry.

Yet, actually, transformation did not seem impossible. He had heard too many stories of actual cases to be too sceptical. When he was a child there had been a sorcerer near Artois, an evil man who, aside from making all the ordinary potions, could transform people into stone. Blondel had been too frightened ever to visit him.

Wenschloss was several days in the past and even vaguer in his mind when the strange forest ended abruptly and a brown and desolate plain began. Far in the distance he could see grayish hills edging the plain and, in the center of the plain, like some strange yet natural growth rooted in the bleak earth, a large village with pointed roofs, dust-colored, with streets which from a distance appeared black. Behind the village stood a castle of dingy, much-weathered stone. It seemed very old and, except for the contemporary ramparts, much of it could have been Roman; though why Rome should have wanted a fort in this dead region he did not know. He wondered how the village lived, for the soil didn't seem rich enough to farm.

Since it was already late afternoon he decided he would spend the night here, perhaps at the castle.

The cold afternoon sun was in his eyes as he rode down the streets; the sky was violet with evening and from the forest behind him he could hear the wind starting. He stopped in the village square and watered his horse at the fountain. Several people were in the square and they watched him with surprisingly little interest. They were pale, unhealthy-looking people, he noticed. But then almost anyone would be unhealthy in such a place. Then he noticed an odd thing: the church on the edge of the square was ruined. One door was broken off and the other hung on one hinge. Part of the roof had caved in and Blondel could see debris piled in the nave. It looked as if lightning or some terrible wind had smashed only the church, leaving the rest of the town untouched.

"What happened here?" asked Blondel, turning to an old man, the person nearest him. The old man was deaf and Blondel repeated the question; the old man obviously heard him this time but he looked away.

"Who's lord of the castle?" asked Blondel loudly, in an angry voice.

"The Countess Valeria," said the old man, and he looked at Blondel with yellow eyes. "And she'll like you, my lord, my hearty lord." And the old man started to laugh, but no sooner had he started than he stopped, as if someone had put a hand across his mouth.

Blondel mounted and rode towards the castle. A countess.

Well, he always got on better with women than with men. This countess should be no exception. He presented himself to the guard at the gate, a gaunt, pale man who seemed surprised to see him but, asking no questions, led him into the castle. A servant showed him a room and told him the Countess would receive him at dinner.

There was definitely something strange, Blondel felt, about this castle; for one thing, there was so little noise. Usually castles were full of shouting and clanking, the noise of children and dogs. But this castle was silent. Servants walked noiselessly in the corridors and there were no children anywhere. As the slow hours of the evening passed he grew more and more uneasy and afraid.

The castle was not large but, with few people in it and those few almost noiseless, it seemed immense. The corridors looked like tunnels in a granite mountain. The great hall was like a cathedral's nave, and as cold. Torches lit only one end of the room, the end farthest from the fire, and here, on a dais, seated in a chair behind a table, sat the only other diner.

The Countess Valeria appeared to be tall; she was also slim, too slim. Her face was as white as new milk and her eyes were hidden in blue-shadowed sockets. She was not young and yet she was, apparently, not old either. There were lines about her mouth but the shape of her face was young. Her mouth was a dark red, wide and heavy-lipped, quite unlike the rest of her face, which was thin and delicate. Her hair, like smooth copper, glittered dully in the light. About her head she wore a silver circlet set with a single cat's-eye. She was antiquely dressed in a white tunic with gold designs. She nodded to him when he bowed.

"You are welcome to my castle," she said. Her voice was low and, for a woman, deep.

"Thank you for your kindness, Countess." He introduced himself.

She motioned for him to sit opposite her. It was strange, certainly, to be dining with only one other person in the great hall of a castle. Servants brought them food and wine.

Three minstrels sat in the dark, out of the circle of light, and played what sounded to Blondel like oriental music, high and thin, dolorous, wailing music.

"And does the crusade continue?" asked the Countess.

"Why no, not at the moment. Richard signed a three years' truce with Saladin. Most of the crusaders have returned, I think."

"Richard? Richard who?"

"King Richard . . . of England," said Blondel; she was joking, of course.

"I thought Henry was king of the English."

"No, he's dead."

"I see. We're beyond the reach of ordinary travelers, you know, news comes slowly. It was years before we heard of the death of Duke William. He was a friend of my brother's; in fact, my brother was with him when he entered England."

"But . . ." Blondel stopped himself; the woman, obviously, was mad. That explained everything. The silent castle and even, perhaps, the sullen villagers and the smashed church. Yes, she was mad; almost one hundred and thirty years had passed since William invaded England. He smiled at her; he would charm her. "Those were great days," he said and then he asked, politely, "Where is your brother now?"

"Dead," she sighed and glanced at her white hands, long-fingered with pointed nails like the claws of an alabaster dragon. "All of my family are dead except my father and me; he lives in another part of Austria, an out-of-the-way spot like this. Our family has never cared much for the life

119

of courts. We live privately," and she laughed softly, dry leaves rustling: "but do tell me of the courts. I'm always curious about what's happening and some day, soon perhaps, I'll leave this castle and travel again. I haven't left this place for many years now. I think Frederick was Emperor the last time I did. But I don't suppose the world has changed much: a few wars, new kings, and those ridiculous crusades. I disapprove of them, you know. They're quite useless." She said this last with sudden feeling; her voice for the first time rising. "But take more wine," she said, resuming her ordinary inflectionless tone. He poured himself wine from a silver flagon, red wine, like garnet.

"Do you like the music?" she asked.

"Yes . . . odd music, almost impossible to sing to, I'd think."

"No, one couldn't sing to it. The music comes from Asia; my minstrels are from Asia, too. I like the sounds, though, don't you? Like wind." And as she spoke Blondel heard the wind begin to sound about the castle. Gusts of it swept through the hall and the torches flickered and smoked.

"Yes, like the wind." He looked at her and saw she was smiling and watching him. He wished he could see her eyes, tell what color they really were, their expression, but they were hidden in deep shadows. "Your forest," he said, "was rather unusual, I thought."

"Really? In what way?"

"It was . . . too quiet; all the trees were twisted out of shape . . ."

"But I like the quiet, don't you?"

"Not that kind, no. Is the forest enchanted?"

"What does 'enchanted' mean? If you mean has magic been made in the forest, yes. But there are so many kinds of enchantment and some are unnoticable. Magic creates and magic, certainly, destroys or transforms. Some magic can be performed only at night, in league with the devil; other kinds are performed at noon. Some enchantments last only the life of a single full moon, while others endure until stones powder to dust and forests die." She looked at him and he wondered what to say. He had understood nothing of this. He wondered if she could be making a spell now, for the way she spoke was reminiscent of incantation. Behind her voice the Asian music wailed.

"But you believe in spells?" he asked.

"In some kinds, of course. Not in others. It's simple, certainly, to enchant someone, to make another obey, to put another to sleep. Many people can do that: with words, with their eyes or light flashing on silver. I've been told that it's possible to make gold, but that has never interested me. If one has power, why make gold? Then, the magic of the potions is simple; any old countrywoman who understands herbs can make potions for lovers or for murderers. Many spells, much magic, but only one great spell after all."

"And that is . . . ?"

"The one of life."

"To live forever? No one can do that."

She shook her head, smiling. "There are a few of us who will; a few who have already lived past their age, who live secretly, at night. We must live at night, or the sun hurts our eyes and withers our skin: the moon is cooler, a borrower of light and, in that, like us."

Yes, she was quite mad. He would agree, though. "I have heard of such people," he said.

"Everyone has." She put her hands on the table; the nails glittered in the light of torches. "Everyone knows us. Children fear us in the dark and dogs cry when we pass. The wind is our ally and even lovers feel our chill at night when we pass below their windows in the street. We understand time, you see. The passing of hours means nothing to us: days and months are all alike and the years are so many heartbeats for us . . ."

"Then you cannot die?"

"Never by ordinary means; not from decay, at least, not from age. Lightning could kill us, a fire in the forest, a mountain exploding or a river's rising: only those elements separate from the human touch us."

"You must be lonely," said Blondel, watching the long-nailed fingers.

"Lonely? are hills lonely? is the forest lonely? is the moon lonely? We are like stars, single and apart, set to endure forever; what could the human give us?"

"I don't know," said Blondel. "I don't know what you are or what you need."

She laughed. "I have no needs. I shall remain here until the stones in this castle are sand; only then, perhaps, shall I arrange to die."

"You would like to die?"

"There are times when I should like to sleep, when I should like to go back to darkness with no mind, no memory, no dreaming, only the soft earth about me, the cool dark earth. Yes, there are times when I should like that. One can grow weary of the days, weary even when time has no real meaning, when the passing of the day means nothing, no change, only another period of light to be followed again by a period of dark, another moon and the familiar stars. But centuries do pass for the people outside the enchantment, and it's amusing to watch new kings make new wars and then to see them become only bits of memory and distorted fact while their sons reign, only to follow the fathers. And, beyond all this, I remain unchanged while change occurs in the world."

"You prefer to belong outside the world?"

The cat's-eye shone brightly; the room was growing darker. Something was happening. The Asian music wailed thinly, part of the nightmare wind.

"We're all separate," said the Countess, and her voice, too, sounded distant. "Each alone; I merely endure for centuries what mortals endure for years. During the days I sit in my room in the tower. The windows are shuttered against the light; only one torch burns; I sit in my room and remember the years, the centuries that I have lived. Then, at night, I go into the village and search. Or, perhaps, go into the forest to cast spells. Oh, the nights are beautiful in the forest! The branches twisting and the wind shrieking like a great bird among the trees. No moon can shine in the forest, no stars shine: a part of the enchantment, you noticed. Yes, I often walk at night in the forest."

The cat's-eye was becoming brighter; there was no doubt about that; the music ended. Her voice was like a voice in a dream. He tried to move, to look away, to escape the vivid eye, but his head would not turn and he must watch it now until he ceased to be; until the world became nothing but one bright eye surrounding him.

Finally he moved his head. It took a great effort to move, but he did at last. Light circled behind his eyelids; small brilliant cat's-eyes, hundreds of them, all glittering, watched him.

Then he opened his eyes. He was in a large room. Tapestries hung on the wall; over his head the ceiling was supported by carved beams. Two torches stood on either side of a heavy chair and here the Countess sat, smiling, her eyes as pale as winter ice. She no longer wore the circlet with the cat's-eye.

He tried to move but discovered that his hands were tied behind him, tied to a low bed on which he lay. He felt sick and exhausted.

"Did you sleep well?" she asked.

"Did I sleep?" His voice sounded weak in his own ears.

"Yes, you slept all the night and now it is day, almost night again."

"I'd like to get up."

"Not yet, not yet. You must rest awhile longer. You must still be tired."

"Oh . . ." This was too much. He shut his eyes; at least he wouldn't have to look at this insane woman. He wondered why he was so tired. Of course: he had been drugged. Without thinking, he began to test the ropes which tied his hands. They were not tight. Carefully he began to loosen them even more. As long as he wasn't moved from this bed he had some chance of freeing himself. He opened his eyes again and looked about the room; his clothes were piled in one corner with his viol. Then, wearily, he shut his eyes and worked on the ropes under him.

"You feel tired, don't you?" the Countess remarked.

"Yes." He moved his head so that he could see her. When he moved his head he was aware, suddenly, of a sharp pain at the base of his neck. "What happened?" he asked. "What's wrong with my neck?"

She smiled and then he understood; his heart almost stopped beating as he realized what she'd done: she had taken his blood; she was killing him. He shivered.

"You . . . you'll do . . . this again?"

She nodded. "In a day or so."

"And I'll die?"

She nodded again. "In a few weeks. But it will be so gradual that when the moment comes you will think it only sleep.

Perhaps you will live three weeks since you seem strong."

He shut his eyes and went to work once more on the ropes.

"Are you hungry?" she asked. Then, without waiting for his answer, she rang the bell and one of the silent servants appeared with a tray of food; obviously all of this had happened many times before and the man had been waiting for her to ring. He lifted Blondel's head and began to put food in his mouth. Blondel, hungry, ate what was fed him. She talked to him all the time.

"More and more I find I need strangers like you," she said. "My village is old and the people in it are too inbred, quite unsatisfactory, and, of course, I can't let them die; so I go from one to another at night, secretly, and they never know I've come until the morning when they see my mark upon their skin. I'm told they hate me in the village but don't dare rise against me for fear of magic: wise of them, certainly. Only a few, actually, ever die because of me. Only strangers serve me completely."

Blondel shivered: the room was cold. "May I have my cloak at least?" he asked.

She shook her head. "Why? In a few days it won't matter if you've been cold or not."

The servant finished feeding him and, at a gesture from the Countess, disappeared.

Then she rose, slim and tall, a pillar of green like seawater frozen. "Now I shall leave you. The few hours I'm gone won't seem long to you. This room is outside time, and in an instant I'll return." She left the room.

But the room was not outside time and he was aware of what had happened and what, very certainly, would happen to him if he remained for long in this room. The food had made him stronger; the weariness had passed. He worked with his fingers on the ropes: they were looser already. He wondered if all she had said was actually true. Was she really some sort of sorceress, living forever? the vampire, not dead and not living? If she was not what she said, then she was insane: a murderess, with a need for blood. Fear made his mind quick and his fingers sure; he was not going to die in this place; he was not going to die like this. He thought of what he should like to do to her. Elaborate tortures occurred to him: fire and pincers and the rack, water tortures with Saracen variations; oh, he should know what to do to her. But, perhaps, it would be better just to strangle her, to choke her. Yes, he would like that best; to choke her until the body went soft and heavy in his hands. He almost wished she would return after he had freed himself. Fear had become rage and he was strong.

With a great effort his arms were free. He stood up and, for a moment, a green cloud blurred the room; he was afraid he would faint. He held his head down until the room was clear again. He felt the loss of blood. Then he rubbed his wrists until the blue marks of the ropes were gone and he warmed himself at the fire. His skin looked white to him, corpse-like. He rubbed himself vigorously, made the blood run faster, then quickly he dressed. His viol and his purse were both untouched. Ready, he looked about the room for doors. There was the main door through which the Countess had left. Near it, half hidden by an arras, was a smaller one. He was about to try this door when he noticed a jewel box on a table beside the Countess's chair. He opened it and took out a fistful of jewels: rubies and emeralds in silver and gold settings. He stuffed all that he could into his purse and, smiling to himself, bolder than he had ever dreamed he could be, he opened the secret door.

A semi-dark staircase, as steep as a well: he stood on the top step and shut the door behind him. He waited for a moment until his eyes were accustomed to the dark. Then, able to see a little, carefully, without a sound, he descended.

For a long time he crept from stair to stair, feeling the rough irregular stone under his feet. There were no windows, not even slits for the archers in the walls. The light from the bottom of the staircase, a gray wisp, grew bright enough to cast his shadow on the wall. He could see clearly now; he reached the bottom of the tower. A door was open and a torch stood beside it. He could see the back of the guard to the left of the door; in front of him was the village square. This was undoubtedly the Countess's private entrance. He had a sudden picture of her, smiling, her eyes ice-bright, moving silently down the steps of the tower, towards some evil, bloody adventure.

Blondel drew his dagger. It was all so easy: flesh entered – a long sigh and a clatter as the man fell. Swiftly Blondel stepped over him and into the square. The air was bitterly cold. The stars were out. He ran through the streets, the sound of his own footsteps sharp and clear in his ears, the only sound in the night.

He ran until the forest was all about him, until he felt protected by the inhuman trees and even the noise of the wind, hissing and whistling in the branches, seemed a friendly sound. Safe among trees, he slept that night, dreaming of gardens.

6

One day of travel and the wind no longer blew at night and the forests were alive with small animals moving. It was cold and the winter was preparing one final chilling blow before the days grew longer and the ice melted, before the rivers began to roar again.

He found it difficult to travel fast at first; he was weaker than he had suspected and he was afoot now with no opportunity to buy a new horse until he came to a town, and there were no towns on the way to Durenstein, only villages and few of those. He no longer visited castles or, if by chance he was forced to stay at one, he asked about the owners from people who lived near by. He wanted no more experiences like his last. He could barely wait to leave this forest-marked and silent land of magic, to go from night to day, from the pale winter sun to the brightness of summer and the west.

Now he knew, instinctively, that he was outside the circle of enchantment. The villages he passed were concerned with the problems of ordinary living. Each night by firelight he examined the jewels of the Countess Valeria and he chuckled to himself, watching the light sparkle on the stones: cold clear jewels, hard and brilliant like the eyes of kings. He wondered what she had done when she discovered he had taken her jewels; had she been furious? was the village searched? He thought of what he should do with the gold he would get for them. He would buy lands in Picardy; perhaps build a small castle. He made plans for the future, for his life when the King was restored. Days passed; his strength came back and he was well again.

On the old Roman highway to Durenstein, during the last few days of his journey, he met Brother Antonio, a monk en route from Italy to a monastery at Durenstein. Since Antonio was good company, Blondel traveled with him; both were on foot and the time passed more quickly talking. He no longer wanted to be alone; he was afraid of being alone for the first time in his life. He needed to feel that there was someone else, some sort of security, no matter how slight or imaginary.

They slept the first night in an inn, Brother Antonio and he; the next day they woke early, ate much, fastened their cloaks tightly and stepped on to the highway.

There were more travelers on this road than Blondel had seen since he left Vienna. Knights in full armor followed by servants and squires clattered along the road, riding as if they were late for battles which could not be won without them. Monks traveled, too, generally in pairs, their hoods about their faces and sandals on feet which looked cold and no doubt were.

The countryside was bare, stark and severe and, fortunately for travelers, flat. The trees were thin and sharp and looked as if they had never borne leaves, would never blossom again, the sap frozen forever under hard bark. A pale mist hung from the branches, blurring the outlines of the distance.

Brother Antonio, small and sallow, moved agilely; his eyes were black and shiny, onyx eyes. His face was thin and his nose was long and straight. He spoke French easily if not well and Blondel enjoyed listening to him. As he spoke he gestured vehemently with long yellow fingers, black-furred and broken-nailed.

"We hear such stories in Italy but only legends, of course. No one I've ever met has seen such a person, except, of course, yourself. It's possible, certainly, that your Countess might actually have been alive for centuries. Those who go in league with the devil are often rewarded materially and she was, there's no doubt about it in my mind, in league with the devil. You know this is one of the devil's strongholds, this part of Europe. Magic is still practiced here and I've been told of transformations, of werewolves in the forests. An evil country from all accounts, though the people seem reasonably devout. I've even been told of an actual entrance to hell in one of these forests. This *might* explain the unusually large attendance of dark angels here. I should like very much to see that entrance but I suppose the soul would be seriously endangered.

"Strange, strange country. Look at it." And he gestured at the flat, iron-colored fields. "Looks as if a curse were on it."

"But this is winter," said Blondel reasonably. "I hear the land is quite beautiful in the summer."

"Beautiful, perhaps, but sinister still, I think. In pagan times the witches gathered here on the mountaintops, thousands of them, riding eagles; they performed the Black Mass at midnight, and the devil, like smoke and fire, appeared among his servants." Brother Antonio shuddered and crossed himself at the thought.

"Do witches still meet, I wonder?"

"They say they do but no one knows for certain. I'm sure your Countess would have known."

"Do you have them in Italy?"

Antonio gestured, spread his yellow fingers. "I expect so, in certain parts, but I've had no experience with them, only hearsay. I'm told there are evil spirits in Rome itself."

"In Rome?"

"Oh yes, among the ruins. You know we have all sorts of ancient ruins there, almost covered with dirt, most of them. There will be no peace until they are buried; that's my theory, but the Popes have thought otherwise and there's even talk of restoring a few of them. Heaven forbid! Of course, a few pagan temples have been made into churches with no ill effects – so far; but I think centuries of wickedness can't be erased except by the earth and time or, where possible, consecration."

Blondel listened to him as he spoke of the old days before the Church; he wondered what life was like then. The pagans must have been remarkable; their roads and their walls, their aqueducts and temples were still visible all over Europe, still used. Generally, Blondel disliked priests. They usually spoke with such false righteousness, maintaining always a sacerdotal infallibility which he found both irritating and questionable. On the other hand, they had saved old books and taught people to read and that was, certainly, good. He himself had learned to read from a priest in Artois, a tall gentle man with a deep voice and curious eyes. But all of that had been so many years before. He had never known another priest as well.

Now he walked beside Brother Antonio, listening to stories of Rome. Thieves went openly in the streets to the city. The cardinals lived in great luxury and there was much intrigue over the Papacy. It all sounded too familiar: this was the age of insecurity, of warring factions, of the individual against the men who wanted large central states. Ever since Blondel could remember, there had been trouble in the world; small wars between small states; kings murdering one another. There seemed no direction in the world except, perhaps, at Rome, and he knew, of course, even before talking with Brother Antonio, that Rome was like any other political center, as full of intrigue, as directionless, moving as blindly towards the mystery as the other states.

Well, none of this really concerned him although he had a certain memory, an atavistic one perhaps, of a time when there were no small wars, no intrigues, a period of sunlight and quiet, when one could move safely about the world, when there was no fear. At times, in the pagan era, the world had been like this, or so he had heard; the roads had been new and they connected every part of Europe and all lords obeyed the government of Rome; now the roads were old, grass-covered many of them, and the stones were broken; it was difficult to get from one city to another and people were hostile to strangers. There was no longer a center point, a single authority; the father had died and the sons warred.

"These are evil times," said Brother Antonio as though he had only recently discovered this condition. "And yet I don't see how man can be intentionally wrong. Hell is certainly a frightening thing and most believe in hell."

"I think the difficulty is in the definition," said Blondel. This was something he had thought about. "We really *don't* know what good is or what evil is. We're directed, more or less, by the Bible, but only priests and a few others can read and the priests, certainly, haven't been living examples of what they preach. Then, good and evil change their meanings from age to age, from country to country. Men don't really think seriously in those terms since they don't understand them; men do very much as they must and they must eat, make love and, sometimes, fight. I think that's probably the way life was meant to be and all the rest of it is a suggested method for living, necessary, perhaps, for the general comfort, for the physical security all of us want, but not in itself final truth."

"This sounds like heresy," said Brother Antonio worriedly and he looked at Blondel to see if he meant what he said; he was not reassured. Blondel meant what he said even though it was seldom that he spoke as honestly as this. Usually he accepted the contemporary hypocrisies as gracefully as anyone.

"Perhaps it is heresy," agreed Blondel.

"How can you say there is no good and evil? This Countess you met, *she* was certainly in league with darkness; you said as much. Don't you feel she was evil?"

"Not evil in your black-and-white, absolute sense. She was dangerous to me because she tried to kill me in a particularly terrible way; but she needed, or, at least, she believed she needed, to kill me. I might say that that would have been evil for me but not, necessarily, in an absolute sense. It would have had no relationship with the stars, for instance, or Leopold's court. This concerned only me. Yes, I should like to have such people as the Countess killed for my own safety, yet not because I consider them abstractly evil but because they threaten me. I quite agree that if we are to have some sort of order we must impress the ignorant and the dangerous with all sorts of tales about a god whose only concern is to take elaborate personal revenges, to sit in judgment. But let's not believe our own political myths. Regard them merely as laws for our protection. I seem to remember that King Richard was applauded by the Church when he killed a few thousand Saracen prisoners. The Church condoned it and yet a crazy woman like the Countess Valeria is considered wicked because she tries to bleed one man to death! How unreasonable."

"Sophistry," said Brother Antonio, horrified, "all untrue. Reason has nothing to do with faith. It's because our understanding of spiritual matters is so limited that, sometimes, our reason seems to contradict our *knowledge*. Faith exists independent of what we call our reason. It is wrong and arrogant to suppose that our minds, because they draw conclusions different from the Church's, must be right. Some things we *know*, those things are beyond reason and we must not question them since they are true."

No sensible answer had ever been made to this. They all spoke this way. He wondered if there were schools where churchmen were trained in this sort of argument, taught to distort reason, to ignore contrary evidence, to discuss paradox as an illusion of the devil. Well, perhaps they were right; perhaps it was better to accept the nonsense and try to believe it, better never to think of such matters as good and evil, only obey the instincts when it was possible, compromising as little as possible with the world. They would all die soon and what any of them did would make no difference, would not affect the rising of the sun, or the cold light of a single star.

They walked together, talking. Evening and sunset, round orange sun, a bitter wintry color: streaks of yellow light across the hills and fields. The air was still; the wind was gone, whirling now across some other country. They talked no more of religion once Brother Antonio had discovered Blondel's numerous heresies. He was shocked, Blondel saw, for Rome, powerful and rich, politically so important it could make an Emperor walk barefoot in penitence, the Church at Rome, entrenched in its dogma, maintained, with some reason, that this was the age of faith. No one dared question the Church openly and Blondel had only dared speak now because he knew he could always later deny what he had said in the presence of one person; besides, he would soon be out of Austria. France, the land of the troubadours, was not, at least at courts, as priest-ridden as the countries of Central Europe and the Mediterranean. And then, basically, he did not question the Church's authority. He merely found its attitude towards morals curiously paradoxical and, considering the practices and instincts of human beings, often absurd.

They talked of love as the orange sun failed.

"Men never love women, nor women men," said Brother Antonio darkly. "They experience lust, certainly; the flesh against the spirit with the flesh, alas, dominating all too often in this world."

"But you wouldn't suggest men never taking women, would you? There'd be no race then, no good and no wicked, no priests even."

"Procreation can be accomplished without lust," said Brother Antonio serenely. "It should be performed as a sacred duty rather than as a source of pleasure – the motive, unhappily, of most people."

"But just why don't you believe a man could really love a woman, for instance?"

"Love a woman in the actual sense? a great emotion, a selfless emotion directed towards something outside oneself? No, that can only be experienced between man and God. Love as affection, as friendship, as physical lust, is, of course, quite possible between men and women."

"What is it then when a person is so in love with another human being that when he looks at other people he grows impatient, not finding the lover's face among strangers? What is it when a man thinks of a woman every minute of the day, loving her, obsessed with her and, at night, dreams of her? What is it when a man can risk his life for someone else, no longer considers his own life important compared with his loving: what is this?"

"Madness and sin," said Brother Antonio.

"Yet it happens to men, not many, I agree, but to some."

"Did it happen to you?"

"Once, yes, I think so. Once, a long time ago," and Blondel thought of the first woman he had ever loved, a lady of Artois. With an effort, he tried to recall what he felt for her. Though he could remember certain scenes, all colored with the light of summer, he couldn't quite recall the sensations of great emotion; rather he remembered only words: the descriptive words of loving came to him, words which were, at the most, only common empty shells of meaning, relics of

135

emotion, the debris of loving. Perhaps Brother Antonio was right: only lust, but if so, then what *was* love ? Words were so puzzling the more one studied them. How simple it was to sing the word "love," to use the word "heart" in a ballad, to speak of languishing, and yet the peaks of emotion could never be viewed in memory; the pain and the delight became words once the instant passed, and when one was not actually loving, love did not exist. Yet while one loved, the moment quite consumed the mind, existed beyond, most probably, the understanding of men like Brother Antonio.

They decided, finally, that they did not agree.

Now it was night, and before them, lumps of black under a moon, was the town of Durenstein; the light of torches shone in the narrow streets and there were lights in certain castle windows. His heart beat more quickly; he could feel a familiar tightness in his throat. He had come out of the wild witch country, and, for a time, he would be in a great castle among the civilized and here, he was almost certain, he would find Richard.

They stopped that night at the large monastery of Brother Antonio's order. The stone buildings were two stories high and there were many courtyards and outlying buildings. A chapel was still under construction; it stood now, jagged and unfinished, a confusion of stones arranged against the night sky.

A servant led Brother Antonio and Blondel into the chapel, where the monks were gathered at service: it was midnight and they were performing matins, the first service of the new day. It was a solemn scene, thought Blondel, who had seldom visited monasteries: the monks all praying together in a roofless chapel, the light of candles flickering crazily in the drafty aisles. There, when at last the service ended, Brother Antonio presented himself to the Prior, a stout white-bearded man.

"You are welcome," said the Prior to Blondel. "It's not often that troubadours spend the night with us. They're generally made more comfortable at the castle." The Prior smiled. "Come to the refectory and have something to eat."

They sat, the three of them, in the long refectory, alone, their end of the table lit by a single candle; a sleepy servant served them bread and cold meat.

"What news of Rome, Brother Antonio? We've had no one from Rome for many months."

Brother Antonio told them the news of Rome: the activities of several cardinals, the health of the Pope. He was not as frank, Blondel noticed, as he'd been on the road. Then, events described and gossip told, he handed the Prior a number of sealed papers from the head of the order at Rome.

"These are for the Abbot."

"I'll see he gets them later. Now, troubadour, where have you been? From what place to what place do you travel?"

"From Palestine to France."

"A crusader! Then you are twice welcome here. We have the greatest respect for the crusaders. You represent the strong arm of our Church, the selfless dedicated warrior. The Prior cleared his throat and his voice rumbled grandly: this was undoubtedly a familiar though always piquant theme.

"How I should like to have had some part in your glorious work! The freeing of the tomb of our Lord from the Infidel, to be joined with the greatest soldiers in the history of Christendom! Oh, how lucky you've been! How you will be envied when you return to France by those less fortunate, those who've never fought in the Holy Land; how I envy you! If I had not been so old, so tied down by my duties to our order, I should have been present at St John of Acre myself. Well, each of us must perform his work for the Lord." His voice trailed away impressively. Blondel looked at the remains of cold mutton on his plate and the Prior stroked his beard gently, his eyes vague with dreaming and with age. "Tell me," he said in a different voice, "how were the spoils at Acre divided? We've heard so many conflicting stories. You *were* at Acre, weren't you?"

"Yes, I was there. But I'm not sure exactly how the spoils were divided; mostly between Richard and Philip, I think."

"Duke Leopold got very little, then?"

"So we were told; I have no idea whether it was true or not; there was so much looting . . ."

"They say the Saracens are very rich," said the Prior a bit wistfully, combing his beard, loosening knots in it.

"Exaggerated, I think," said Blondel, "but we took everything they had at Acre. And, I'm told, Richard took most of the spoils himself."

"We've heard that," said the Prior and he smiled secretly, a smile almost lost in his beard. "They say Duke Leopold was greatly distressed but I feel it was his own fault; he should have been stronger in his dealings with Richard. He should have known that all the Plantagenets are dishonest. Things would have been different if our Emperor had been there."

"Why wasn't he?"

"What? Well, he has too much to do in Germany, and then Duke Leopold represents him, you know; Austria is part of the Empire, as Leopold discovered." Again the secret smile which Blondel understood perfectly well; perhaps not the details of the secret but certainly its nature.

"Leopold and Richard have never been on friendly

terms," said Blondel, wondering what to say, whether to ask directly or to wait.

"Richard is a disgrace to Christendom," said the Prior and he frowned fiercely, fumbling with a particularly difficult knot in his beard. "He's an assassin; he murdered Montferrat, you know: a Christian lord and a better one than Richard himself. Then, after taking the lion's share . . . that's what he should be called instead of Lion-Heart . . . after taking everything he could get his hands on, he makes a peace with Saladin and leaves Palestine, deserts our cause! Imagine a Christian king dealing with that infidel, Saladin, that slaughterer of Christian knights!" And Blondel tried to look as if he were imagining all of this, as if, imagining it, he was shocked. This obviously was going to be the Emperor's case: desertion, conclusion of a personal peace with Saladin and the murder of Montferrat, not to mention seizing too large an amount of the treasure at Acre. He wondered how the Emperor would present his charges, under what pretext, and also when. Nothing had happened yet, or so it appeared; if there had been a trial the Prior would certainly have been full of news. The Emperor was probably having difficulty setting up the machinery for trying a king since he himself was too responsible a statesman to ask for ransom outright. There would, undoubtedly, be a trial of some sort. Blondel wished he knew what was happening in England; was John King yet? he wondered. It was quite possible Richard had been proclaimed dead. He thought of all that could be happening in England. But what was the Prior saying?

"It happened months ago in Vienna. They say the Duke Leopold himself seized him, that Lion-Heart had disguised himself as a cook but that Leopold recognized him and defeated him in a hand-to-hand contest. Then the Emperor demanded Leopold give Richard to him and I hear there was much ill feeling (as you can imagine); but Leopold was forced to obey. I've been told there will be some sort of trial before the Diet, but that takes time and I suppose there are many international problems to be considered. Personally, I should think it a very difficult and dangerous thing for one country to try another country's king, even though we're so obviously in the right." He paused, considering the right, then turned to Brother Antonio. "Have you any idea how Rome feels about this?"

Brother Antonio shook his head. "No, I don't believe I heard anyone mention it in Rome. I think, perhaps, one of the documents I gave you for the Abbot may say something about Richard; but I'm not sure. Personally, I think it's a very foolish thing for the Emperor to have done, considering that Richard, no matter what his sins, is in the Pope's favor."

"I'm sure he won't be when the Holy Father learns the details of his conduct in Palestine. There are limits, my dear Brother, to even Christian patience. Well, it's late, or I should say early, and you want to sleep. You'll sing at the castle tomorrow, troubadour?"

"If they ask me."

"I'm sure they will. I understand Richard has his way about everything. The Lord of Durenstein is terrified of him and, though his lordship hates singers, they have dozens of them in attendance and, I've heard, there's gambling and Heaven only knows what else going on there. If he were my prisoner I would certainly be more severe, but then I suppose they must be careful."

A servant carrying a torch led them through the cloisters, a shadow-shattering spot of flame before them, an eye of fire; they followed the torch across the main courtyard to the guest hall.

That night Blondel didn't sleep. Instead he watched the black sky become gray, then white, and he saw the sun rise, vivid and new; he watched the light glitter on the snow and he thought he heard a noise of birds returning from the south, but perhaps he only imagined this for the sky was empty. So much of his life had seemed unreal.

Day and the sun shone within coldness, shone upon the white crust of the snow. Day and, moving for an instant between the hard earth and the yellow sun, a flight of birds flew across the sky and into the sun.

III

The Return

Spring: 1193

1

The castle was large: a jumble of many crenelated towers, of tall brown buildings and miles of thick wall. At the last moment he was afraid. What if he were recognized? what if the King were gone? it was possible he'd been moved again. He almost didn't want to know; better to stand forever in front of this castle, this pile of brick, stone and wood, and believe that it contained the King and, believing this, be happy.

He stood for a time memorizing every detail of the brown weather-marked castle, the sun burning his face; the day was warm and the snow was melting on the earth; there was, at last, a suggestion of spring in the air: the slow, the ugly death of winter had begun.

"Troubadours are always welcome these days," was the guard's remark.

"You'll be able to sing tonight for a very distinguished guest," said a plump man in the courtyard, leering.

The courtyard was full of men-at-arms, an unusual number for peacetime; they were, no doubt, needed to guard Richard. The Emperor was probably (and rightly) uneasy about his prisoner; he had every reason to be, thought Blondel, walking among the soldiers, watching them as they polished bits of armor, wrestled and laughed together. The courtyard was brilliant with the colors of their tunics; red, green and blue, and the sunlight was reflected blindingly sharp in their metal armor. There was a continual sea-like roar of talk, broken occasionally by the snorting or whinnying of horses.

He walked among them, unnoticed and ignored. There were so many strangers here that one more made little difference.

He walked through the crowds of men towards the main keep. Then, looking as though he were on some urgent errand, he went inside, down a corridor, through the great hall, through galleries and corridors full of servants chattering, until at last he was lost; he didn't dare ask anyone the way out. Still looking preoccupied, he wandered along the stone corridors, glancing at the rooms, passing no one except servants and an occasional guard. Finally he chose a door and opened it. Sunlight dazzled him and he stepped outside.

He was in a garden, a long walled garden; several bare trees grew against the wall and, in banks, brown bushes grew, now flowerless, frozen, awaiting their proper season. The garden was deserted. On one side of it was a high wall and on the other a square tower, part of the main building of the castle. The windows were slits, no more; this castle, guarding the marches of Europe, was designed for the protection of the West from the East; heavy walls resisting, it seemed, a continuous seige. He walked about the garden, ran his fingers over the rough walls, touched the brown and brittle twigs of the frozen bushes. Then, idly now, he sat down on a stone bench, gathering his cloak under him like a cushion for the stone was cold; he played his viol and hummed to himself. He was humming an old tune of Provence when a lady appeared in the garden. She was middle-aged, a little stout, pale-faced with the gentle expression of a rabbit. Her cloak was thick and lined with fur. He stopped humming when he saw her; he stood up and bowed.

"Who are you?" she asked, surprised.

"A troubadour, a stranger to your castle." He introduced himself.

"I'm the Lady of Durenstein," she said, and he began immediately to mumble apologies but she stopped him.

"This is the private garden of the ladies of the castle. It's really *quite* forbidden, you know," she said archly. "But of course you're a stranger and wouldn't know. Tell me, though, what *are* you doing here?"

"I was composing a ballad, Lady."

"Oh, really! Then I should never, never have disturbed you. I should hate to think that I had interrupted a ballad. I know just what it must be like to make up songs; one should have absolute quiet so that one's feelings, one's words will flow. It's so important that everything flow, don't you think? I mean that there are no serious interruptions to things. My son writes quite a few songs. I should love you to meet him sometime. He's really quite good, we think, his father and I. But rather a shy boy, I'm afraid. And, I expect, a disappointment to his father; he has no gift at all for swordsmanship, but then the sensitive type never does, or so I've found. I'm sure he should have gone into the Church or something like that, but we felt that that was really too morbid a life for him. He's in Vienna now, at court. We hear he's been brilliantly received, which is so important, I think, for anyone who has to be a lord some day. He spends part of his time in Vienna and the rest of his time with the Emperor. So you see he's very seldom here. They tell us the Emperor's taken quite a fancy to him and likes to have him sing for him. Such an honor for a young man! I'm sure that *that* pleased his father. The Emperor has so few favorites, you know. But then our son is so sensitive and so quick to understand. Really at times more like a girl than a boy and, by the way, he used to come in here to compose his ballads; we always let him have the garden all to himself when he was here. So, as I say, I know just how it is. Where did you say you were from?"

Blondel told her. She was a most amiable woman, foolish but kindly; he was glad he'd made a friend at court so quickly. He told her his usual story. She listened politely but her eyes wandered absently about the garden, looking, no doubt, for signs of change, for the first marks of spring.

"How nice, then, that you've been able to visit us here. We like troubadours now (*I've* always liked them), but this is the first time we've ever had a great many here."

"Why so many now?"

She sighed. "You'll learn tonight. We have a very distinguished guest, a very famous one, in fact, staying with us." She sighed again. "King Richard is stopping with us."

"Not Lion-Heart!"

She nodded unhappily. "Yes, we're very much honored to have him with us. Though it's a rather difficult situation; for us, I mean. You see, everything must be exactly the way he wants it and he wants so many things. At least a dozen troubadours in attendance all the time, and then there's all the gambling and the drinking with the men-at-arms . . . oh, it's very difficult having him with us. Not, of course, that I mean to complain," she said quickly, afraid she had said too much.

"How long will he stay here?"

"Ah, that's not for us to decide. It's hard to tell and he's such a nice man, really . . . I think." She talked a great deal of Richard's charm and then, shivering a bit, for the day was turning colder, she said, "But I must leave you absolutely alone while you compose; I hope tonight you'll be able to sing us an absolutely *new* ballad."

"I hope so too, Lady; I shall dedicate it to you if I may."

"That will be nice," she said and she smiled at him, still a bit absently, and, glancing once again at the bare branches of the trees, she left him.

Suddenly happy, he began to sing, his voice loud and clear in the still air. He sang several stanzas of one of his own ballads. Then he paused, took a deep breath, about to sing the *envoi* when, from far away, a voice made resonant by echo, a familiar voice, answered him, singing the *envoi*.

The words died among echoes. He stood quite still. He looked up at the tower but he could see nothing but narrow slit-like windows set deeply in rough stone. Yet it was true; he had heard Richard's voice again and that was enough. The journey, for a time, was over. He had sung and he had been answered. Certain for the first time in months, relieved and happy, he left the garden and wandered like a sleeping man through the corridors of Durenstein.

He sat far down the table with the men-at-arms, jugglers and other troubadours; none of these last were familiar to him. They were the usual sort of troubadours one found in this part of Europe: the delight, no doubt, of secondary courts. He had difficulty keeping his eyes off the main table, for here, flanked by the Lord and Lady of Durenstein, sat

Richard. The King was paler than he had remembered and his beard had grown fuller. Under a scarlet tunic the outline of his body seemed thinner. Almost everyone in the room watched him, they were awed and a bit frightened.

"And he pushed the guard who was in full armor down the tower staircase! Such an awful noise! especially with him laughing all the time . . ." One of the men-at-arms told this story at Blondel's table, while the others listened, nodding as though they had heard such stories before. They looked curiously at the King, who sat quietly at the head of the table; the lion feeding.

The Lady of Durenstein nodded amiably at Blondel when she saw him and he bowed into his plate. The Lord of Durenstein was a red-faced man in his sixties who very likely had a considerable temper himself, controlled now, though, for Richard dominated the room.

Only once during dinner did Richard look at Blondel; he looked him in the eyes, his face expressionless; then he looked away. Blondel heard a pulse beating in his ears.

The blue eyes were the same and the world was the same again.

Time was not and all was fixed, constant and immutable.

"What does the Emperor plan to do with him?" asked one troubadour of another. The other, a man of some information and, obviously, of even more opinion, told him. "They say there'll be a trial but I doubt that. I expect he'll hold the King for ransom and get whatever he can out of the English. Anyway, that's the story. But *I* have another theory. I can't tell you where I heard it but my source is most authoritative, a person of state; according to *him* the Emperor is already in touch with Philip in France and John in England and both have offered him many marks to dispose of Richard and let John reign . . ."

"What has the Emperor decided?" asked Blondel, interrupting the other, barely disguising his anxiety; he had, of course, no respect for the other man's opinion but anything might be true and this story was logical and had even occurred to him.

The well-informed troubadour glanced at him irritably and said, "*I* certainly don't know. I don't suppose anyone knows yet. Obviously the Emperor hasn't made any decision since Richard is still here. The Emperor never hurries, you know; it's a tradition of his family – and a wise one."

The troubadour nodded to himself, pleased both with his sentence and the Emperor's family; Blondel nodded in return, gravely, accepting this information as accurate, as superior to anything he might know.

"Well, no matter what happens," said a young troubadour, leaning forward and watching Richard as he spoke, "they'll always be afraid of him. I'll bet that if they decide to kill him they'll use poison. I can't think of any executioner who'd dare touch him."

"What about the Pope?" asked Blondel.

The well-informed troubadour stared at him coldly as though he'd made, if not a rude, a disagreeable remark. "No one knows," he said, as though that answered the question.

"But that is the problem, I've heard," said the young troubadour, a pleasant young man with orange hair and a freckled face; he seemed Richard's partisan. "The Emperor won't make a move, that's certain, unless the Pope agrees, and I'm sure the Pope won't allow him to kill Richard."

"I've heard that, too," said Blondel, looking at the well-informed troubadour, who, though he had so little information to offer, nevertheless spoke carefully, the guardian of large secrets: "The Emperor's the favorite of

the Pope since he's the first prince. If I were the Pope . . ."
and here the troubadour unconsciously straightened Papal
robes, frowned beneath the weight of three crowns and told
what he would do if he were Pope: obey the Emperor.

Blondel lost interest; he glanced at the head table and he
saw that Richard was telling one of his involved indecent stories. He could tell this by the expression on his face and by
the expressions on the faces of the others. The ladies turned
quite pale and looked away. Richard gestured as he talked;
the blue eyes bright, glittering wickedly. The men looked
embarrassed; the Lord of Durenstein turned a darker red
and played with the heavy rings on his fingers. The men
laughed, finally, when Richard finished and the women
smiled while Richard's own laughter, hoarse and loud,
sounded in the great hall; everyone laughed too, in imita-
tion: the jackals answering the lion.

Suddenly Blondel began to sweat; his armpits were wet
and he felt a trickle down his left side; he was afraid to sing.
It was his most terrifying moment since the first time he
had sung at a court, years before. He trembled and composed his face, yawned to relax himself, but the fear, the
inexplicable fear, remained. He was afraid that his voice
would break, that he might not even be able to get the first
words out of his mouth. He murmured them to himself: he
must sing, his voice must be right, but still he trembled and,
for the first time in many years, an audience frightened
instead of stimulated him. He wondered desperately what
had happened, what was happening, and, cold and trembling, he listened to the other troubadours sing. Raimond of
Toulouse was announced and for a moment he didn't recognize the name; then someone pushed him and he walked
through the confusion of faces and sound, presented himself to the Lord and Lady of Durenstein, bowed to Richard

and, without thinking, his conscious mind paralyzed, he began to play. The first chords of music froze the world, made everything stand still, become vivid and sharp; then he was aware that he was singing. At first his voice was tight and constrained but, when faces separated, when the confusion of color and sound ended, his voice became clear, more certain, and soon he could feel it rising strong and unobstructed from his chest and echoing back to him from the corners of the room. He sang at first to the Lady of Durenstein. Then he sang a song of an imprisoned heart, and he looked directly at Richard as he sang; the King's face was expressionless.

When he finished there was great applause and, though they asked for more, he refused to sing again. He was weak, wet with perspiration; when he sat down at his own table and took a goblet of wine, his hand shook so that the wine spilled all over him. Suddenly, in the midst of congratulations, he heard Richard's voice. He glanced up and saw the King was standing, speaking.

"Such fine singing has inspired me," he said, smiling, and Blondel recognized his dangerous smile and wondered what he would do now. "I should like to entertain my generous hosts with a ballad of my own." The Lord of Durenstein half rose from his seat in protest but Richard touched him on the shoulder and the Lord of Durenstein resumed his seat abruptly.

A servant handed Richard a viol and he sang. He sang of treachery, of the courtiers in England who had deserted him, who had let him remain in prison; he sang out their names one by one; he attacked his captors and no one dared stop him. The audience sat shocked and helpless. Huskily he sang the *envoi* and the last bitter words were almost snarled. No one made a sound when he finished. The Lord of

Durenstein had turned alarmingly pale for such a red-faced man. No one dared applaud and Richard sat down, looked about him, laughed suddenly and, in a loud voice, demanded dice and thus broke the spell. The room was filled with the sound of indignant talk.

Richard looked at Blondel only once: he nodded and smiled and, for an instant, the blue eyes seemed really to see him. Then Richard looked away. Blondel knew what he must do; he understood the danger. The direction was clear and he could move again, move from the center: certain, at last.

2

He rode from Durenstein. He had sold some of the Countess Valeria's diamonds and, well harnessed and supplied, he rode towards the west, to the greener softer hills of France, rode out of Germany, out of the haunted forests.

For a week he rode. He rode alone, stopping at castles, at inns, passing the night, often, in the forests. He crossed great rivers full of breaking ice and he stood on tall hills and saw lakes like silver mirrors, saw brown forests and, where men lived, he saw the dark and broken earth of their fields. The towns were small in this part of the world; the buildings huddled close to one another as though afraid of the forests, of nature more than men; the people were quiet and spoke slowly, calm dark men, related to their landscape.

Then he rode through a region of lakes, and on the banks of one of the lakes he watched the winter go as ice on the lake broke and birds wheeled in the sky; the sun shone brightly and the air was warm. He watched this lake for nearly an hour one afternoon. Then, contented, he moved on across the land, leaving no mark, no scar.

The second week he came to a large city beside a river. Many churches touched the pale blue sky and, since it was a Sunday, bells tolled, a rich and antique sound. The people smiled as they walked in the streets, strolled with one another, arm in arm: there was a lightness here, related partly to the coming of the spring, but more, perhaps, because the forests of Germany ended at this river's bank and here began a happier or, at least to Blondel, a less strange land.

He walked down a narrow muddy street, listening to children shouting, to the laughter of women and to the talk of men. The square was wide with an elaborate fountain in the center. Many people strolled about the square; a fair-haired people in a shadowless city, moving brightly in the sun.

He sat awhile on the rim of the fountain, watching: his horse, a patient bay, stood near by, tied to a stone marker.

"You're a stranger, aren't you?"

He looked around and saw a young man standing beside him: a youth with light yellow hair, straight silk-like hair and slanted hazel eyes; he was smiling.

"Yes," said Blondel, smiling back.

"I thought so; you look different. People in a town can always tell a stranger. Where are you going?" The boy sat down beside him; Blondel had forgotten what friendly people were like, what it was like to talk to a stranger and not anticipate danger.

Blondel told him where he was going and, more or less, where he had been. The boy listened to him: he was sturdily built, clean and pink with large red hands; his tunic was neat but old.

"Oh, that's the life," he said when Blondel had told him a little about the crusade. "I've heard stories before, of course. I come to the fountain a lot when I'm not working in my father's place (he keeps an inn). I can talk to travelers better here than I can with him watching me all the time."

"How old are you?"

"Eighteen – just. I wanted to serve in our Duke's Guard; that's his castle over there." He pointed to a group of towers in the east, above the roofs of the town. "But my father won't let me so I work around his place; I do almost everything. What's your name, by the way? Mine's Karl."

Blondel told him his name, his real one. The boy looked at him with surprise, respect. "You're not Richard's Blondel, are you?"

Blondel laughed. "I didn't know they called me that."

"I've heard a lot of your songs. Almost every troubadour who comes here sings some of your ballads and tells stories about you and Richard."

And Blondel, who liked praise, listened happily as Karl told him his own legend. Listening, he thought what strange things people said about one: the stories they invented, the characters which, for good or bad, they created from their own need; the facts were relevant only if they fitted the convenient image, a frame to support the stuff of the legend. He found that the figure described was not much like life, more like a dream character, a being which reflected all that its many creators lacked, demanded but never saw in reality, could never realize in the light of their personal day. So he listened to the story of Richard and Blondel in Palestine, listened to a large-eyed boy who watched him, who saw, instead of a troubadour tired from many journeys and not young, an enchanted maker of ballads, a king's friend and a witness of battles. Blondel was suddenly sad as he realized that he had been, indeed, all of these things the boy described; he had wanted to become what the boy maintained, according to the legend, he was. But, since he lived continually in the enveloping present, lived in reality, experiencing fear and pain, he had had no time to consider what he was as a human being, what he might mean to others, to boys who lived in pleasant cities beside great rivers, cities where Richard was known to be the instrument of a war god and Saladin to be the devil's agent. He wondered if this long journeying would ever come to an end; if he would ever be able to sit and consider the fact of his own living, to recall events beyond the immediate boundaries of emotion . . . He sighed. It was no use. He was like a fragment of ice in the river, touching other fragments, moving rapidly, helplessly with the river, and slowly, inexorably dwindling until at last the final dissolution, water into water, river into sea, life into death and, perhaps, death into something else – all, however, within the current, flowing with the river, always in motion, governed by the moon and the tides.

"Don't you feel all right?" asked the boy. "Have you had anything to eat yet?"

"What . . . oh, yes, I feel all right. I'm a little tired, that's all. I've been traveling several months now. Yes, I'd like something to eat."

"Good, you can come to my father's place. I don't have to work Sunday afternoons, sometimes; but I'll take you back there anyway. He'll be pleased to have you in his place."

The father was a thin and angry man; respectful, however, of money. Blondel, the only traveler of importance in the inn, was given a room to himself. He had dinner early, before the other travelers ate. Karl served him. Then, tired, he went to his room; he had come so far. He lay on his back, the small window above his bed partly open; he listened to the faraway sound of bells ringing, the sound of all the Sundays of his childhood.

He awoke suddenly. Moonlight poured in through the window and the room was bright with silver. He frowned, trying to think where he was: then, remembering, he was about to close the window and shut out the moonlight when a voice said, "No leave it open."

"Who's that?"

"Karl. I hope you don't mind. I know how tired you must be but I have to talk to you."

"What about?" Blondel sat up in bed, his back against the rough-wood wall. The boy appeared from the shadowy corner and stood in the moonlight. He looked quite unreal, like a silver statue fashioned in a classic age. He stood beside the bed, looking down at Blondel; then he said, "I want to leave here and I'd like to travel with you, if you'd let me. I don't have any money but I can be a help to you; I'm very strong and I speak French and German and I like to fight. I wouldn't be afraid of danger or anything like that; at least not very afraid, and then I know how to cook and when you're traveling that's important and . . . well, can I go with you? Please."

Blondel smiled at such earnestness but his smile was invisible by moonlight. "But what would you do when I reached England? I'm not going to be traveling forever, at least I hope not."

"Oh, I'd get into Richard's army and go off to the crusades. That's what I really want to do. I mean I want to travel with you very much, but I'd like to go to Palestine, too. You haven't any idea what it's like living in a place like this where nothing ever happens or at least hasn't happened in my life, where you have to see the same people every day and hear them say the same old things."

"I know what it's like," said Blondel and he thought of his own boyhood in Artois, thought of it with longing, wondered if, ever again, he could live the way he had as a boy, the way Karl did now: secure, contented, caught in a familiar rhythm, surrounded by people he had always known, people who could neither surprise nor threaten him. He envied the boy but he said, "If you want to travel with me you're welcome to; but what about your father? what will he say?"

"Oh, he won't know till I'm gone." He paused. "I'm so glad you'll let me go with you. You'll never know just how much I wanted to leave this place . . ." The boy stopped. With no more words he stood glittering in the moonlight; then he sat down on the bed.

"I even have a horse," he said.

"I was going to ask you that; is it your own?"

"Well, in a way. My father said I could use it when I wanted to . . . he's got several, you know, so I think it'll be all right if I take it. He's never given me anything for working in the inn and I've worked here ever since I was a child. But I think we'd better leave very early."

"Yes, that's a good idea: I steal his son and his son steals his horse. He'll probably be angry."

The boy chuckled. "I'd like to see his face," he said. Then, "We'll have to leave a little before dawn. Father wakes up then but I'll be awake before him; I always get up first. Oh, it'll be so wonderful . . . seeing the cities and traveling with someone."

The sky was still dark when, as quietly as they could, they rode away from the inn, down narrow empty streets and through the city gates into the flat country beyond the river.

They did not speak until day. The sky in the east turned from black to gray, a pale and dingy gray. Then all the sky went gray and the wind stopped blowing. Diaphanous red edged the horizon and, as they watched, ribbons of it blew across the sky while, behind the colored light, the sky became clear and, swimming in color, the sun rose and it was day again.

"I don't think I've seen the dawn in a long time," said Blondel, his own voice ending the stillness, putting an end to night and, for a time, obscured a silver vision.

"I watch it every morning," said Karl, loosening his cloak in the sun. "I can't imagine what it'd be like to start a day without watching the sun rise."

"Do you feel different yet?"

The boy nodded, smiling, white even teeth: "Yes, already. I'd be cleaning out the stables now if I was home. It's just the way I thought it would be, riding like this. Nothing to do but watch the cities pass and cross rivers."

Blondel laughed, pleased, as though he had invented traveling himself, pleased at the other's pleasure. "There's more to it than that," he said judiciously. "After all, we're going somewhere and you have to think what you'll do when you get there."

"But I thought troubadours just travel, never stay anywhere very long."

"In a way maybe that's true, but this time I've a place to go and work to do. After that . . . well, that all depends on so many things. I never think too far ahead anyway."

"Neither do I," said Karl. And he began to sing and, to Blondel's surprise, his voice was good, true and rather deep. They sang together and Blondel taught him many songs and he taught Blondel a few of the songs sung in his town.

Blondel was happy. Not for many months had he felt relaxed, secure: to be with someone he liked, to talk when he felt like it, sing when he felt like it or, if he liked, to keep silent for hours, comfortably aware of a companion. Karl was a perfect companion; he knew instinctively when to be quiet and when to be gay and he watched after Blondel, preparing food when they were in the open country, arranging with inns when they were in towns. They came to Paris, and Karl marveled at the size of the city, admired the great churches on the island of the city and the palaces on the banks of the Seine. They spent only a day in Paris; a day was long enough for Blondel to hear that John and Philip Augustus had made an alliance, that Richard was assumed, officially, to be dead, that England was split between Longchamp and John.

They rode through country beginning to green. Small yellow-green blossoms on the branches of the trees and the snow turning to water, turning the black earth to mud. They rode towards the sea, stopping as seldom as possible, avoiding cities, taking the most direct route.

Late one afternoon, when the sky was pale and the evening star was the only star in the sky, they saw the sea before them, gray in this light, disturbed by a sharp wind which stung their eyes and smelled of salt.

3

"There he is, over there." The seaman pointed to a fat man, wearing the hooded habit of a monk. The fat man was watching the coast of France become sea-mist. Blondel motioned to Karl to stay where he was; he joined the man.

"They tell me, Sir, that you're the Bishop of Salisbury."

"Uh . . . yes, yes, I am." The Bishop looked at him; his eyes were light and filmy, contrasting with his features which were sharp and clearly cut, in contrast, again, with a large and shapeless body.

Blondel introduced himself and the Bishop looked surprised. "I thought I recognized you. I heard you sing in London when you were there with the King. You were with him in Palestine, too, as I remember."

"Yes, I was there; I was with him when he was captured, too."

The Bishop motioned to a bench near the bow. "Sit down. Longchamp sent me to find what has happened to him . . . It has been rumored in England that the King is dead. But I learned from a knight I met in Paris that he was still alive."

"Did the knight give you my message?"

Salisbury nodded.

Blondel told him the story of the capture and of Richard at Durenstein. He asked why the knight hadn't gone to England, hadn't delivered the message sooner.

"He told me the reason but I'm afraid I've forgotten; he was having some sort of quarrel with his family, I think, and he wasn't able to return immediately."

"And I thought everyone in England would know by now Richard was a prisoner." Blondel was exasperated.

"In a way," said Salisbury, "we did know he had been captured but there were so many stories it was impossible to know which were true. At first we heard he had been shipwrecked and drowned. Then some of the company who'd landed with him . . . at Zara, wasn't it? got back to England and so we knew he hadn't been drowned; then we heard Leopold had taken him captive. We were about to send an embassy when Prince John announced he had been informed Richard was dead. Since then there's been nothing but confusion in England, and I expect John's already King in certain parts of England, in fact if not in name. Longchamp and the Queen are in London trying to hold the country together. Longchamp sent me to Europe a month ago to find out exactly what had happened. As it was, we didn't have to go much further than Paris when we met this knight of yours and also, through spies of mine at Philip's court, we learned that the Emperor had taken

Richard from Leopold . . . is that correct? Yes? and that John had known of all this for some time."

"Doesn't the Queen have any control over John?" asked Blondel and, as always, he meant Eleanor of Aquitaine, not Richard's wife.

Salisbury shrugged and shifted his position on the bench. "No one has control over people with armies. The most the Queen can do is to try to keep civil war from breaking out, to keep John away from London as long as possible."

"Then you think there'll be a civil war?"

The Bishop nodded sadly. "Yes, I think there will be a war. How long it will be delayed no one knows, until Richard is back, I hope. You didn't have a chance to talk with him at Durenstein, did you?"

"No, but we understood one another; we sang."

"I wonder what his advice would be now."

"I think to get him out of Germany as quickly as possible. He believes, I'm certain he believes, the English know he's a prisoner already and, because of John, they're doing nothing to free him."

"Well, we shall do a great deal now. Longchamp will send an embassy to the Emperor to learn the ransom . . ."

"But what about John? what about the treaty with Philip?"

"You've heard about that, too?" The Bishop's eyebrows curved like the wings of a gull in flight. Blondel nodded.

"That's the most difficult part of the business," said Salisbury, picking his nose thoughtfully. "I don't know just what the treaty is or even if there is one. There's been, certainly, some sort of understanding and I expect it will mean another war with France, sooner or later. We'll probably know this month what Philip and John have agreed to. We have quite an involved information service in Paris, quite involved." The Bishop smiled complacently.

161

"Do you think there's any chance of sending an army after Richard?"

The Bishop shook his head. "Not a chance in the world. Even if we could raise one, we'd have to send it through France and then through Germany, two hostile countries. And if we did raise an army the Emperor could very easily threaten to kill Richard . . . no, I'm afraid this problem must be left to the diplomats and politicians."

"Which will take time," said Blondel irritably.

"We're just as anxious as you to recover the King," said Salisbury, fixing his pale eyes on Blondel; "quite anxious, as a matter of fact, but we have to move carefully. We must avoid mistakes."

"You know the King is furious," said Blondel.

"We appreciate that," said Salisbury, gesturing defensively, "but it takes time to make a plan and more time to act."

"Have you any idea what Longchamp will do?"

"Well . . . actually, no. As I said, I expect he'll send an embassy immediately and ask for terms."

"Nothing else?"

"What else?"

"He could go to the Pope and ask for his help; he could imprison John . . ."

"No, no, no," said Salisbury, thoroughly shocked. "What *are* you suggesting? The last thing we want is a civil war now. John has considerable strength among the barons, considerable strength. We wouldn't dare touch him yet. No, only Richard himself can deal with him; it's not for us to touch the King's brother. The best thing we can do is delay and maintain what we have."

So that was the policy. Blondel was not surprised. Many times he had listened to Richard lament the lack of imagination among his advisers and their inability to act. But

Richard had been able to shape his own policy and he had selected Longchamp for Justiciar chiefly because of his amenability. Now he would have considerable leisure to regret his choice; Longchamp would act slowly, if at all.

Salisbury stood up, carefully bracing himself against the motion of the ship. He gathered his robes about him. Blondel noticed that he was quite pale and his hands trembled. "I'm afraid," he said, "that I must lie down for a while; the sea . . ." He walked away quickly and Blondel laughed.

He was alone on the forward deck now. The Bishop's retinue was out of sight and so, for that matter, was his own Karl. He looked at the sea, looked at it hopefully as if it were one of those magic mirrors which show the future; but it showed him nothing, indicating only fragments of the past.

Color: gray, with streaks of white and, if one studied the sea closely, a dark, a vivid blue under the gray, under the streaks of white foam, the foam like a fisher's net thrown on the sea. The ship cut through the gray, scarring for an instant the smooth and shifting surface of the water.

Air: gray and the sky not quite white, pale with a thin sea fog but full of salt and sharp when the wind blew in gusts down from the northern sea. Gulls, gray as the air, as the sky and the surface of the water, flew and shrieked, whirled in the wind like conscious omens, swooped to the surface, rode waves and flew again.

Already the French coast was out of sight and, ahead of him, behind the mist, hidden by distance as well, was the coast of England, that green island which Richard ruled but seldom visited. None of the Plantagenets had much liked living among the English. Richard had spent only a few months in England although he had been born there at a town called Oxford. Blondel himself had visited England only once, at the time of Richard's coronation.

Soon afterwards they had left for the crusade.

His face was cold and damp with spray but he watched the mirror, could not leave the sea-framed images of the past.

The grayness of Amelia's eyes was caught in the seadisk. What of her? The night before the fire, the warm still night where there was no sound but the fast and regular beating of their hearts. What would have happened if he had insisted she come with him? Leave the forest country and come with him to the cities. He knew. He would have grown tired of her. In time she would have ceased to interest him and she never would have understood the manners of courts; she would have grown old, her face severe, critical, and her eyes would look at him without understanding or sympathy and they would live together, silently, growing older, each waiting for the other to die, waiting without real hope for that release. All this would, he told himself, have happened but if he could have her now . . . a wave broke white and the gray eyes vanished in the white.

Richard at Chinon receiving the news of his father's curse, a dying man's curse, with a smile. He thought of the strange man he had searched for all over Europe and he wondered what Richard felt about him, about anyone; Richard who never noticed people. No one, it seemed, could touch him and yet he could remember times when Richard had looked at him as though actually aware of him, had smiled or gestured or said a certain word as though in answer. Yes, there were times when Richard had seen him and, for those times as much as for future moments, he could not regret his search for the King and all the days gone.

Richard, Richard, Richard.

The sea repeated the name, waves repeating it endlessly. The name was carried from wave to wave from France to England and back to France again.

He thought of dead men, lost at sea. He could see ships sinking, imagine this ship sinking: the cold water all about him, drawing his body into it, crushing air from his chest, stopping the heart. He would float swollen on the surface and then, after a time (how long a time?), he would sink to the floor of the sea, lie among the slime-covered shells of ships, lie with other bodies, Roman and Viking and Norman, lie there forever in an attitude of sleep among the forgotten drowned.

Now he was cold. The sea gave him no more pictures, no longer mirrored the past or murmured names. The water was a gray circle at whose center rode the ship, watched by gulls. He drew his cloak tighter at the neck. He rubbed his face, warming it; then he left the deck and joined Karl.

4

William Longchamp, Bishop of Ely, Papal Legate and Grand Justiciar of England, was not happy. He sat at his table in the long cold room, wearing a thick cloak of fur, spotted with tallow and the remains of several banquets. He was a thin man: his neck was bent as though he wore an invisible yoke and his face was puckered and lined, green-tinted with illness, perpetually frowning. He coughed often into his hand or, occasionally, into the fur of his coat. His fingers were bent and ringless and they gripped a pen as naturally as other men's gripped a sword's hilt. The wood table in front of him was spread with rolls of parchment; another table behind his chair supported several thick books. Though it was noon no daylight entered the room and the only light came from several candles beside Longchamp's chair. Two men in dark tunics, green-faced, out of sympathy no doubt with their master, secretaries, moved about in the dim light carrying papers and writing in books.

Longchamp motioned to them to sit on a bench beside him; the light shone full in their faces while his own was obscured, against the light.

Salisbury, dressed in church robes, spoke first and Blondel listened. Longchamp frowned and coughed and fingered the rolls of parchment.

"You see," said Salisbury, finishing, "there is almost no question that the Emperor is holding the King for ransom."

"I know, I know . . ." Longchamp gestured irritably, obviously bored by Salisbury's attempt at interpretation. Then he turned to Blondel. "And what did the King say to you?"

"We didn't speak at Durenstein."

"Did not speak? I thought you were in the castle?"

"I was, but there was no chance to speak. I understood him, though."

"How was that?"

"By singing. He sang a ballad he had written and it was easy to tell what he wanted, what he felt."

"I presume I know what he wants," said Longchamp sharply. "No doubt he wants to be released. But what, in your opinion, does he feel about the situation?"

"For one thing, he is angry with the English nobles and he thinks they have done nothing to rescue him. In fact, in his ballad, he attacked them by name."

"Well, we can't do any more than we have done," said Longchamp scowling, looking at Blondel as though he'd been the one to accuse the nobles. "There are many other things to consider; the situation is delicate and we must move carefully. After all, we haven't known officially until this moment that the King was still alive; there was nothing we could do until we knew exactly where he was and what was expected of us by the Emperor or Leopold . . . whichever held him. Let me say, though, we've been busy." He touched a pile of parchment. "These are all reports concerning the King. Collected rumors, drafts of messages to the Emperor, to Philip in France; oh, we haven't been inactive . . . no matter what the King thinks, we have done all we could. His Majesty has always been impatient. He has never appreciated the difficulties and the delays of negotiation." Longchamp looked unhappily at the documents on his table, each one representing, no doubt, a difficulty and a delay.

"Now what have you heard of the Emperor's intentions? Any rumors?" He looked at Blondel for the second time during the interview and Blondel looked away: the man's face was alarming in its ugliness.

"Not much. I heard only a few rumors . . . I got an impression, though, that the King would be tried by the Emperor."

"I heard that, too," said Salisbury, importantly. "In Paris it was said . . ."

Longchamp glanced at him and Salisbury stopped abruptly. Blondel went on. "I believe they're going to fix the amount of ransom at the trial. And I'm quite sure that they won't harm the King until then."

Longchamp nodded, coughed. "So am I, unless, of course, we send an army for him as certain of our advisers would have us do, as, I am sure, the King himself would have us do. No, we must continue to negotiate. I shall send an embassy to Germany at the end of the week and, I think, perhaps one to King Philip."

"I heard," said Blondel, interrupting Longchamp, aware of his own tactlessness, "that Philip and John have signed some sort of an agreement, have made a treaty."

Shocked, Longchamp looked at him. Salisbury, too,

167

seemed alarmed. "There are always such rumors," he said at last, distantly. "We know how to handle them. Prince John is in England now; I don't see how he could have signed anything with Philip recently." Longchamp looked at him blandly as if what he had just said was not only profoundly reasonable but also true. Then the Justiciar rose and they did also. "You may stay here as long as you care to," he said to Blondel, almost kindly. "And will you attend me tomorrow, Bishop?" he said to Salisbury, who said that he would, murmuring elaborately, as they withdrew.

They parted in the corridor and Blondel went through vast stone rooms to the wing of the castle where he and Karl lodged. Their rooms were comparatively cheerful: the walls were hung with new tapestries, and at this moment yellow sunlight streamed, mote-filled, into the room.

Karl, wearing only a scarf about his middle, was mending his tunic. He smiled when Blondel came in. "Something I learned to do back home," he said. "I always thought I'd make a good tailor. Had to learn how to do this when my mother died." He bit the thread. "How did your meeting with . . . what's his name . . . the Justiciar go?"

"Longchamp? About as I expected." He pulled off his cloak. The room was pleasantly warm. He lay down on the bed and shut his eyes: glowworms, concentric circles of green light, glowed behind his eyelids; one ankle was warm where a bar of sunlight crossed it.

"Is he going to do anything about the King?"

"Oh . . . eventually, yes; but he'll take forever." He rolled his head back and forth and the concentric circles faded into red darkness.

"What are we going to do now you've seen . . . Longchamp?"

It was always "we" and, to his own surprise, he liked it,

liked belonging, even in this casual fashion, to someone else. He was needed and it was odd to feel needed. He knew that, at times, Richard had needed him as a companion, but for Richard there had been so many companions and Blondel knew he had never really been needed until, on his own, he had set out alone to find the King: a journey back towards the center of his life. Now, however, unasked, this boy had attached himself to him, shown his own need. Emotionally, without thinking, Blondel had responded, the periphery touched and perhaps even more. He glanced at Karl, who was now energetically beating dust out of his tunic, the sunlight was thick with swirling dust.

"I don't know," he said. "Maybe we'll stay in England for a while. I should see more people, I think. Would you like to be in the Guard?"

The beating stopped. "Do I have to? I mean I'd like to sometime but you won't be in London very long, probably, and what shall I do when you go off to France again? Couldn't I go with you? I'm not much trouble."

He was so serious, he looked so troubled, that Blondel laughed. "We can stay together until Richard comes back. Then you can join his Guard. Maybe he'll make you a knight someday."

Blondel thought of the future. Perhaps he would marry and settle down at court. But better, perhaps, to travel with Richard, who would travel back to Palestine or, more likely, to war with France. He himself could do what he wanted; with the jewels of Valeria he was a wealthy man. They would stay awhile in England, he decided; they would stay until he knew what was to be done about Richard. Then they would join him when he was free, meet him on the Continent and return with him to England.

He got up. For a moment he was dizzy, as he always was

when he got up too quickly. Karl was busily putting on his tunic, adjusting it about himself; sunlight on yellow hair gave an illusion of yellow fire.

"Are you going out?"

"No, I'll be right back; I suddenly thought of someone I should see."

In the corridor he passed one of Longchamp's green-faced secretaries, who, when asked, informed him that the Queen Mother, Eleanor of Aquitaine, was, for the time, in residence at Canterbury.

The fields were bright and the forests, too, were touched with the colors of spring; green dotted the skeletal brown branches of the trees and birds returned, following the light of the sun.

They rode towards Canterbury and, because the day was bright, the sun warm, and green was everywhere, the vibrant green, they sang and the people in the fields who heard them stopped their work and listened. Pilgrims, merchants with trains of goods, and nobles passed along the narrow way to Canterbury.

In the late afternoon the wind, the sharp spring wind, ceased and the sun made them warm. And so, passing through a green wood, they rode off the highway and into the shadowy woods. They stopped in a small clearing where a stream widened into a pond before resuming its narrow course. They dismounted and let their horses graze. Blondel sat by the edge of the stream and, bare-footed now, put his legs in the water. The water was so clear that if there were no current he might have thought he was looking at a bed of rocks, of colored pebbles where, like dragonflies, small fish flashed.

He looked at his own legs, foreshortened in the water: they were pale and the blond hairs turned black when they were wet; he tightened the muscles of his calves. Then he glanced at Karl, who had taken his clothes off and was busily scrubbing himself. He washed himself more than anyone Blondel had known: sometimes as often as twice a week; a habit, Karl explained, he had got from living by a river in a pleasant climate. The sun sparkled on the drops of water which clung to his body. He sang as he splashed about happily in the water, the muscles of his back working, while all about them was the yellow-green of spring, the earth black and soft with preparation.

"Isn't it cold?" Blondel hated cold water; his feet were used to the stream now but he shivered at the thought of coldness. The sea near Artois had been warm the few times he had swum there as a boy in the summer.

"Wonderful! It's clear, too; I've never seen such clear water. At home the river's usually colder than this and full of mud. I never could figure where all that mud came from. But this . . ." he sighed as he splashed a handful of water over his hairless chest.

A bird sang. Blondel lay back and listened to the bird, to the sound of water splashing. He felt lazy, euphoric. He hummed to himself, wondered if he might not make a tune out of the bird's singing.

He opened his eyes with a start; his head had hit against a rock; he had been sleeping. He sat up, stiff, his joints aching. The sun was in the west, a dull orange glow filled the sky. The horses, he noticed, had been tied to a tree, where they stood patiently, shifting their weight from time to time. Karl was gone. His clothes lay on the bank where he had left them. He was nowhere in sight.

Quickly Blondel got to his feet. There were no footprints in the earth, but, curiously enough, there were the new marks of an unshod horse's hoofs on the ground.

Blondel called the boy as loudly as he could. At first there was only silence and the whispering of a wind beginning to stir at the top of the trees. Then he heard, far away, an answering call. He waited impatiently, brushing the twigs and pebbles off his clothes, combing his hair with his fingers. Suddenly he heard a sound of horses' hoofs close to him. He turned around and, for an instant, saw a creature of blinding white with the pink naked figure of Karl astride it and then, before he could identify the beast, before his eyes had become used to the whiteness, Karl had slipped off and the creature had vanished into the woods.

Karl's face was flushed and his eyes shone. "Did you see it?" he asked breathlessly. "Did you see me riding the unicorn?"

"Was *that* what it was? How could you ride it? I thought no one could ride the unicorn."

"So did I but he let me ride him. You'd gone to sleep and I was lying beside you on the rock drying off in the sun when I heard a noise behind me and I looked up and there he was. So I went over to him and treated him just like any horse. I took care of my father's horses, you know. Well, all of a sudden, I mounted him and he was quiet; his coat was just like silk. Then he started to trot very fast and I couldn't control him so I just hung on and we rode . . . we rode all over the woods and it was all different."

"Different?"

"Yes . . . I . . . well, I don't know how to explain but everything was different. For one thing, it was like summer. The trees were full of leaves . . . at least I think they were, and hundreds of birds sang and it was like . . . well, I thought I saw all kinds of people . . . I'm sure I did, too. Some girls sitting in a circle singing, and then I saw . . . but it's so hard to explain. The more I think about it the less I can remember.

That's funny, isn't it? Everything was so clear, too. But you *did* see the unicorn?"

Blondel nodded, disturbed. "I saw it."

"Then I suppose the rest was true, but it's all so funny."

He shook his head, puzzled, and ran his hands through the thick blond hair.

"Are you all right?" Blondel was anxious; this was, obviously, something extraordinary, for few people had ever seen, much less ridden, the unicorn.

"Oh, yes! I've never felt better." And Karl smiled and smoothed his hair, smoothed away memory.

"Well, get dressed then. It's late. We've stayed too long here." They rode out of the woods, seeing nothing Karl had seen.

The garden was small and surrounded by a high wall. Several trees were beginning to green and banks of rose-bushes, ugly and thorned, waited upon the season of roses.

At the end of the garden, sitting in the morning sunlight, was an old woman attended by two young girls who withdrew quietly as Blondel, led by a priest, the Queen's confessor, approached.

Eleanor of Aquitaine had aged since he had last seen her, two years before. Under the veil her hair was white, held in place by a circlet of gold which looked, he thought, not unlike a feminine version of the crown. Her face was long with two deep lines from the corners of the large nose to the chin; her jaw sagged and her lips were thin and pale; her long hands shook. None the less, she seemed in good health. She looked at him with clear blue eyes, with Richard's eyes, and said, in a deep unfeminine voice, "We had heard already you were in England. I'm glad you came

173

to see me; I should have sent for you anyway. Leave us, Father." This to the priest. Then: "Tell me of Richard."

Blondel told her all that had happened. She nodded from time to time but made no comment until he had finished. He stopped with his arrival in England; he didn't describe the meeting with Longchamp, avoided it for now.

"You never heard any talk of Montferrat, did you?"

This was unexpected. "Well, yes and no," he began, trying to think what she meant.

"I mean," she said, "did you hear whether that was to be one of the charges brought against Richard at the trial?"

"Yes, I did hear that that was to be one of the charges, though the main charge was to be signing a truce with Saladin."

She nodded thoughtfully, twisting the gold chain about her neck.

"Do you think," she said at last, slowly, her eyes fixed on one of the trees as though fascinated by it, studying it, "that Richard did murder Montferrat?"

"No, I don't think he did. I know he probably wanted to but he told me someone else had; Montferrat had many enemies."

"So hard to tell what's true; some people claim Richard murdered him and some tell me he didn't. Of course it would make very little difference under ordinary circumstances but these, certainly, aren't ordinary circumstances; but you understand why I must be assured that Richard didn't murder Montferrat: you do understand?" She turned and looked at him so suddenly that he started.

"No . . . I . . . no, I don't."

She sighed and shut her eyes, murmuring, "The Pope: the Pope must be assured." The gold chain tinkled as she fingered it.

"But . . ." He still didn't understand.

"You must say nothing about this," she said, opening her eyes wide, looking directly at him, in a way Richard seldom had. "Since you have done so much for us, for my son and me, I'll tell you: we are preparing an excommunication." She said the dreadful word quietly and with obvious pleasure.

"Excommunication? of whom?"

"The Emperor."

This was too much; such a thing was almost unheard of. It had happened only once before in recent history, and not like this. "Have you heard from the Pope? Has he agreed to this?"

She nodded. "We are only waiting for definite word that my son is still alive and also, I believe, for some assurance that Richard didn't have Montferrat murdered: the Montferrat family is close to the Pope. But now we can act. I'll send word to Rome today and then we'll see what happens. Then we'll see."

Her mouth quivered spasmodically and she covered it with her hand. But since this didn't help she stood up and walked over to one of the rosebushes and pretended to examine it.

"Does Longchamp know this? know your plan?" asked Blondel.

Her back still to him, she shook her head. "Not yet, but I'll tell him presently. I generally invent my own policy and Longchamp generally follows it."

They talked for a few moments longer and then she said, "I hope to see you again soon. You'll go back to London, yes? When Richard returns we'll show you our gratitude but, in the meantime, if there's anything you want . . ."

"No, nothing, Your Majesty."

"I'll see you at London then, in a few weeks. Good luck . . . I shan't turn around."

He bowed to her back and, quickly, left the garden, glancing back only once at the short, rather stout figure of the Queen, still examining a thorny and unleaved bush.

They rode back to London.

It rained that afternoon and they sat under a narrow wooden bridge and watched the rain, sheets of water, slanted diagonally by the wind. The sky was mottled, black and white: terrible phantom shapes, cloud figures, hung over the land and blue-white lightning flashed on the edge of the world and, from the abyss, where the world ended, thunder rolled.

"Listen to that!" shouted Karl, over the noise of thunder. "Listen, listen to it."

"It's hard not to," said Blondel, sourly, shivering, his voice lost in the thunder.

"What? I like it. It sounds like drums."

The drums of an army moving out of the abyss, an army of dark shapes riding over the world with lightning for arrows aimed at the earth, arrows falling and flashing out of the wind. Vague army of vague figures, constantly shifting, wind-guided sun-conquerers, symbols of a strange and large dreaming, the origin of fear: the figures of the ambivalent dead and the final shape of an old terror.

The sky grew darker; the wind hissed wetly in the trees and Blondel watched the waters of the narrow river grow violent. A trickle of water streamed from a crack in the bridge on to his leg. He brushed the water away and shuddered in the cold. He looked at Karl, saw his face clearly in a sudden flash of blue-white lightning, saw he was smiling the way he had the day he rode the unicorn.

At last the army vanished, sinking back into the abyss, and drums sounded no more. The sky cleared quickly and the sun shone again, glittering on the wet grass. The air smelled fresh. A beginning was made, the cyclic renewal.

Blondel stretched himself in the sun until his joints cracked and he wondered if this stiffness came from age or from too many nights spent on cold ground: from exposure, probably; he was not old yet, though there were, at times, disturbing signs: sometimes his heart beat too rapidly when he exercised and his muscles, though still hard, were often stiff, often ached . . . but that was weather, of course. He would not grow old; he would never change and he sang to celebrate this, the permanency of his youth, and Karl, who had never in his life considered such things, sang with him.

They had been in London several days when, one afternoon, a monk, a small cheerful man, presented himself at the door of their room in the castle. Karl was shining a helmet Blondel had bought him and Blondel was sitting beneath the slit-window playing his viol, making a ballad or, rather, trying to make one, for he had found it hard to work in London; there was no center here, no real court: only Longchamp, the secretaries and the bishops: no women, no intrigues and no King.

"Blondel de Néel?" the small monk asked, his eyebrows arched expectantly. Blondel got to his feet; he nodded.

"I wonder if you would come with me? I have a most unusual request. An old friend of yours is in the city. I . . . I was told not to mention his name so I musn't, but he *is* an old friend of yours and he would like to talk with you. He's staying near Westminster and he asked me to invite you. I really can't think why he told me not to tell you his name but . . . well, you know," he smiled ingenuously.

Blondel was suspicious and Karl, simple as he was, frowned, stopped cleaning the new helmet. "I can't think of any friend I know who would send for me like this," he said at last, looking at the little man, who looked back at him innocently.

The monk spread his hands to show, no doubt, that he was unarmed, that there was no blood on him. "I really don't know what to say," he said. "If you don't want to come, there's nothing I can do. I suppose I'll have to tell your friend you refused." He turned to go.

"I'll come with you," said Blondel and he fastened on his sword belt. "My friend here will come, too."

"But I'm afraid . . ."

"He goes with me."

A shrug, "Very well." They walked through the streets of the city, narrow, evil-smelling streets, crowded with dirty people swearing and shouting. Blondel decided that of all the cities he had ever known he liked London the least. More than ever he understood why Richard would never live here.

A few greening trees grew before the large and recently completed Westminster Hall. There were many large new buildings in London, built since the Norman invasion. Instead, however, of going into the hall the monk led them down the side street. He paused at a small gate in a blank stone wall. He knocked, saying, "I think this is the most convenient entrance." Both Blondel and Karl stood, hands on sword hilts, ready.

The gate swung open and another monk, recognizing them, nodded solemnly and stepped aside, letting them pass. A long corridor was in front of them and their monk, their guide, led them down it; Blondel, hearing the gate shut behind him, knew he shouldn't have come.

They were taken to a small room with a single window overlooking a court, a court surrounded by buildings, an anonymous place, lost in the city. The guide told them to wait; then he left them. A table and a large chair were the only furnishings in the room; the small stone fireplace was full of ashes and dead coals. They both went to the window and examined the courtyard, looked for some gate, some way of escape, but there was none; a bare white wall with brown vines growing up it.

"Blondel de Néel ?" a soft voice speaking Norman French beside him. "I am Prince John."

Blondel turned quickly, recognized the Prince and bowed. Karl imitated him. Another man, a bishop by his dress, was with him.

"I haven't seen you in some time," said the Prince cordially. "But I've always enjoyed your songs, always." He sat down in the chair at the table. "This is the Bishop of Coventry, by the way," he said, nodding to the dark, fierce-looking man who stood unsmiling beside him. Blondel and Karl bowed again.

John looked worn and sick, thought Blondel, watching the Prince. The black beard was graying. Lines of bitterness and anxiety broke his face into odd triangles; he was very pale. His hands were as beautiful as Blondel had remembered, long, white, continually moving. Blondel watched him, wondering what would happen, what he wanted.

The Prince told him what he wanted. "I hear you saw my brother, the King, in Germany? Is that right?" Blondel nodded.

"Was he well?" Blondel nodded again. "You have already discussed this with Longchamp, I know. I was also told you went to Canterbury a few days ago: I presume you talked to the Queen?" Since there was still a questioning note in his voice Blondel, for the third time, nodded.

"You know," said John, glancing out the window, "you know that there's a difference of opinion in England as to who should manage state affairs while the King is away. I suppose it is well known that I have always disapproved of Longchamp and, as far as succession goes, I feel that I, naturally, should take precedence. The Justiciar and I, alas, seem never to agree . . ." He talked for a while about politics. Blondel said nothing, remained uncommitted.

Then: "I'm as anxious as anyone that Richard return to England . . . and soon; but, of course, it may take years of negotiation. Years," he repeated, frowning at his thumb as though it had, suddenly, somehow displeased him. "In any event, negotiations must be conducted carefully; we must do nothing rash and we can't threaten . . ." He paused and then he looked at Blondel and said in a different voice, an urgent one, "What did the Queen say? What does she intend to do?"

"I'm afraid I don't know what she intends to do."

"Don't be stubborn, troubadour. Remember that I can have you killed in a second and no one would ever know. I've heard a rumor and I want to confirm it, that's all. Now tell me what she intends to do."

Blondel wondered what to do; he had, certainly, no wish to die at this moment or, for that matter, at any foreseeable moment. He thought quickly, with unusual clarity; then decided. "I don't know what she intends to do now but I think I know what she has already done."

"And what is that?"

"She has got the Pope to agree to excommunicate the Emperor."

John did not take this well. He put one of the beautiful hands, unsteady now, over his eyes, and, gently, he stroked his eyebrows. The Bishop murmured something in Latin.

"Thank you," said the Prince at last, lowering his hand, his face unpleasantly white. "Now a few more questions."

Blondel answered most of them glibly, all of them convincingly. Questions, for the most part, about the capture, about Richard's attitude.

Then John stood up and leaned wearily against his chair.

"As you no doubt know," he said, "I am not supposed to be in London; in fact, it's somewhat dangerous for me to be here at all. I'd prefer it if you said nothing about seeing me, you understand? I could have both of you killed and then there would be no problem, but that would be troublesome and, of course, you're my brother's friend. So I will let you go, but first you must swear not to mention for a week, at least, that I received you in London."

Both Blondel and Karl swore. "We'll see one another again, I expect," said Prince John pleasantly as the two men bowed and left the room.

The cheerful monk met them and led them out. He said nothing and seemed, for some reason, surprised they had been set free.

Outside, the cool air felt good. Blondel was wet with perspiration, his tunic stuck to his back and his face was unnaturally hot.

"Would he really have killed us?" asked Karl, his eyes wide at the thought.

"Oh, yes . . ." As he talked to Karl he thought of what he had said to John, wondered if he had said too much. Probably not, since the messenger had already left for Rome and nothing John might do now could interfere with that. Well, he had done the only thing possible and that was that. In a few days he would tell Longchamp what had happened.

"And now?" asked Karl, picking up a pebble and throwing it at a bird on a wall, missing the bird, hitting the wall. "What are we going to do now?"

"Wait," said Blondel, who had waited before.

THE BATTLE

28 March 1194

1

Spring to summer, summer to autumn; winter and then a new spring and all began again.

They moved about England, listening to rumors, waiting for final news from Germany: talk of excommunication and Europe divided. Then, in July, while they were at Blois, word came that envoys of Richard had met with Philip, that an agreement had been made and that the French King had sided with Richard against John. And, finally, they heard news of the trial.

The valley of the Loire was a dark, dusty green and the river Loire moved like a silver snake through this green. The castle dominated the town, looked out over the river, upon low hills and farmland. Blondel and Karl stayed here all that summer. England was too dangerous for them now; no one knew from day to day who governed and John, it was rumored, had formed an army, was to be crowned King, was already King; Longchamp was deposed, Longchamp was dead: so many rumors.

But the summer bloomed. Gardens with red and yellow and white flowers: a heavy odor of many flowers upon the air, while the sky was filmed over with white clouds, diffusing the blue: a pale gentle color unlike the harsh and vivid sky of Austria. Birds crossed the warm air: tree to tree, garden to garden, darting and gliding, chattering and singing birds.

The heat of the summer was all about them. When no breeze came from the river the air was hot, a cube of heat through which men moved like sleepwalkers. Clouds hardly moved in the sky and, as the summer passed, the sun scorched the green, darkened it, shone on the water, dazzled the eyes; and they spent these days inside the cool stone walls of the keep or else under the trees by the chapel, large trees which cast cool shadows; here in the shade, they could see the river dearly.

Heat and sun: the daily rising and setting among violent colors, earth-scented air and the noise of insects dryly whirring, birds singing and the wind, when it blew, was hot and stirred the dust of roads, silvered the dark green of leaves with dust; all this was their summer and more. They sang as they waited, they made ballads together and sang them at the court of Blois, where they were much applauded. Then, often, they swam together in the river; the two of them alone in the silver water – reminiscent silver. They swam, neither thinking nor remembering, cooled by the river, warmed on the river bank, below the town and beyond the castle. And, lying on their backs, they could watch the pale vague clouds moving slowly like shapeless swans upon the blue and concave sky while a red sun burned its high curve from east to west behind them, piercing, occasionally, the clouds' vagueness, and finally setting fire to them, burning the swans in bright color, a final brilliance before the night, with its black-burned clouds, replaced all the fire and all the light.

They seldom talked to one another when they swam; Karl, red-brown from the sun, would swim swiftly in the river as though obliged to, compelled and even challenged by the water. Blondel, more often, sat on the river bank and watched, not thinking; not even words or pieces of ballads crossed his mind when he was like this in the sun, watching Karl in the water. Even Richard, the center, was remote and he was aware only of the instant, of warmth, of coolness: the odor of flowers, the sound of water, the hard precise shape of his own body, brown from the sun and cleaned by the river.

The nights were dark and warm and the trees made a continual soft noise; insects and frogs made louder noises, a background for human voices, a continual counterpoint.

After they had sung at court they would often walk together among the trees by the chapel. The air of the night seemed almost the same temperature as their own bodies: voluptuous, warm and the wind stirred softly like breathing. Sometimes they would come out here, each with a girl from the court, and they would make love by starlight above the river and, this done, they would watch the strangely regular design of the stars and they'd wonder what stars were.

At other times they would come here alone, the two of them, and sit by starlight, side by side, listening to the night's sounds, barely hearing, from far away, the confused voices of people engaged in living: unreal sounds, voices heard while sleeping, intruding upon the secret personal quality of their star-swarming summer night.

Alone, they seldom spoke; Blondel was aware of nature

with Karl; Karl was nature to him, obvious yet not quite pre-
dictable: natural. He would sit quietly for a time examining,
with Blondel, the pattern of the stars. Then, suddenly, he
would get up and run down the hill towards the river; or,
perhaps he would sing loudly, startling Blondel and waking
the birds. Or he would dance, leap in the darkness, whirl
and lunge, pretend to fight with someone he couldn't see;
then, as suddenly, he would grow tired, hot, and he would lie
down again, breathing hard, damp with sweat, for the nights
were hot and neither the cold stars nor the cool river could
put a chill in the wind or temper the heat. One night, as
summer ended, when the dark green leaves had begun to
darken and curl and a few were bright yellow and some red,
when the wind blew fresh from a cooler place and birds circled over dying gardens where broken roses, rank and
brown, scattered in the wind, birds moving southward again,
they sat together all one night and watched, for a second
time, the morning happen.

Then, as the sun moved into the sky and the night went
wherever it is that the night goes, they went back to the castle while the sun tore, with brilliant claws, the edges of the
dark.

Moving again: from Blois along the river, among the red
and yellow leaves, among the wreckage of flowers and the
stubble of an already old harvest, they moved; the autumn
ceased and winter came again.

They were in Paris for a time and Blondel sang for Philip,
a pleasant man, still in his twenties, younger than Richard,
softer and more handsome and, it was agreed, more cun-
ning than all the princes in Europe. It was at this court they
heard the news.

". . . the Diet is in session and the charges are already
being made against him." The speaker, a plump man, was

just returned from Frankfort. Blondel stood next to him while, a bit breathlessly, he told a group of courtiers what was happening. "He is being charged with the murder of Montferrat, just as everybody said, and also for making peace with Saladin. I'm told they have already decided on the fine . . . ransom's a better word: two hundred thousand marks, and he must recognize the Emperor as his overlord." The plump man then described the trial in detail: witnesses, judges and all.

"How soon," asked Blondel when the man had stopped for breath, "how soon will the sentence be passed?"

"Any day now, perhaps already; but what will take time, of course, will be the English. They'll have to raise the money and everyone knows how they are about money." Evidently the French did, for everyone laughed.

"And now?" asked Karl when Blondel had told him this.

"Back to England."

"There'll be a war, won't there?" said Karl, and Blondel nodded. Karl smiled. "I think I'd like that."

2

In February they heard that Richard was free and then, in March, London heard that he had landed at Sandwich, that John had mobilized an army, that Richard, with an army hastily gathered in France and soon to be reinforced by troops of the loyal barons, was moving on Nottingham, John's capital.

Now, for the third time, they watched the dawn again, Blondel and Karl and a group of knights from London. They had spent the night on cold, frosted ground upon a low hill beyond Nottingham. All night, fires had burned on the hills near the town and the army of Richard, now grown to considerable size, waited for day, for the attack to begin.

Cold, Blondel waited for a new sun to warm him, take the stiffness out of his bones. He hadn't seen Richard yet. No one knew, on this hill at least, where he was. Messengers came regularly from him, however, with instructions for the different captains. There was to be a concerted assault soon after dawn. Now the men moved about, adjusting their mail, standing in the sunlight, warming themselves.

The day was clear. A faint mist hung on the ground but the sky was cloudless and a sharp wind rattled the empty branches of the trees; everyone shivered and cursed the cold. Waited.

Karl was excited. His eyes shone the way they had the day of the unicorn and he couldn't stay still, busy with armor, his horse, his cloak, practicing with his sword, stabbing bushes.

Blondel adjusted his own hauberk, an old leather one, so worn that the leather on the inside was as smooth as his own skin; on the outside it was covered with overlapping metal disks, like a dragon's scales. He felt safe in it, invulnerable but also cumbersome; before the day was over, he would be fearfully hot. He adjusted his chausses; they fitted his legs tightly and were, now, comfortably warm. He left his helmet, for the time, on the ground. His sword and harness he had slung over his saddle. Now he would think of something distracting.

But he could think only of the battle. He wondered how many times in his life he had been like this: fixing armor, waiting for a signal, for the first noisy clanging attack: six times? no, only five. Acre was the worst and the best. The best because there had been little waiting; fighting had begun before they had expected and didn't stop until the citadel fell. Worst, however, because there had been so much killing; the heat had been terrible and the dead rotted quickly in the sun.

He imagined himself, as he always did at these moments, dead. There would be a terrible jolt; the way it had been when he was thrown from a horse as a boy; then darkness. He imagined his body sprawled on the ground and horses riding over him. Then earth over him and he would decay; soon no one would mention Blondel who had written songs everyone sang; he would be forgotten: an empty skull smiling unseen in the ground near Nottingham.

He shivered. The knights about him were thinking of other things, he could see. They were laughing, describing some country girls they'd had the night before. They were short men, Normans, strong with dark straight hair and light eyes. They laughed loudly, helped one another adjust hauberks and swords. All wore dull colors, browns and greens mostly.

Birds chattered in the trees, mimicking the laughter of the knights. Were the others as afraid as he? Was he the only one afraid? Then he realized how calm he must appear to them, how casual, as he yawned and stretched: they were all alike . . . except for Karl, who was never afraid. The boy, tired of stabbing trees and invisible traitors, was sitting on a log by the remains of their fire. He was whistling and drawing pictures in the ashes. He was unafraid but he was also, Blondel remembered, very young and he had never seen a battle. Next time it would be different.

He went over and sat beside Karl.

"How long is it going to be?" asked Karl, drawing the outline of a girl in the ashes.

"Soon," said Blondel. Soon he would feel sick and dizzy, his head would echo with the pounding of his own heart

189

and then, after a moment of this, everything would be precise, simple; he would know what was happening and he
would slash with one arm, defend himself with the other
until his shoulders ached, until the battle, one way or the
other, was decided and ended.

"What's it like, a battle? I've always wondered. I've always
wanted to be in one. I can't believe now it's going to happen. Is there a lot of noise?"

Was there a lot of noise? Yes, he supposed there was.

"I can't wait. Will I see the King? Will he be there?"

"Oh, yes, he'll be in it."

"How can I tell which one is he?"

"You'll be able to tell. He's tall with a reddish beard and
you'll hear his voice all over the field and, I suppose, a man
with the royal standard will ride beside him. If I'm with you
I'll point him out. But you'll see him when the fighting is
over."

When the fighting is over. Here he sat, safe, intact, breathing quickly, aware of the beating of his own heart, the
warmth of his own body; here he sat alive. A bird sang and
the men talked and laughed near him. Everyone was alive.
But down there, down the hill and upon the new-green
meadow before the walls of Nottingham, many men would
die, and, perhaps, he would die, blood staining the grass:
red and green, the colors of feast days. The brightest, most
brilliant colors would mark the meadow where, already in
his mind, he could see the men fighting, could see himself . . . Something tickled his armpit and he scratched
vigorously, wondering if he had lice; did lice leave the body
when . . .

"What happens if we don't win? if something, maybe, happens to the King?"

"What? . . . well, I don't know."

190

That was a new thought. Richard dead at Nottingham and John King.

"Would we go back to France or would we stay here? I don't think John was so bad. I mean he didn't seem as bad as everyone says when we saw him that time in London. And he did let us go, remember? I hope we win, of course."

"So do I," said Blondel, smiling for the first time in many days. Had he been this eager before his first battle? No, no one had; Karl's eyes were bright: the rider of the unicorn. A knight Blondel had known for many years, a friend of Richard's, joined them.

"You'll see him soon, Blondel."

"I hope so. It's been a long time." What else could he say? As a matter of fact, a year, two years was not a long time. He was suddenly angry, irritable, for no immediate reason and so he made himself smile, was genial. "What time does the attack begin, do you know? Have there been any new messages from Richard?" The knight was the captain of their particular group.

"No, same orders; a little after dawn there'll be the sound of a horn and everyone attacks the town. We're to break past those defenses." He pointed to a deep trench before a section of wall. Soldiers of the Prince, archers for the most part, waited here, watching the hills and the woods, the green darkness of Sherwood Forest where, it was said, Richard himself was hidden.

A wind began to blow, sharp and damp with a trace of rain; wind chilled their faces, scattered the ashes of the fire.

The sun rose out of the forest.

"How many troops do we have?" asked Blondel; it was the sort of question one asked a captain before an attack.

But the Captain only shrugged. "No one knows how many Richard collected on his way from Sandwich; a great many,

191

I've heard. Then there's a rumor that a group of bandits have joined him . . . all sorts of rumors. I don't expect it will be too hard to tell when it starts."

"No."

"I heard that old John doesn't have anyone at Nottingham, only a few men." Karl looked at the Captain, who smiled and said, "I expect old John knows what he's doing even if he does lose. He's got enough men there to keep us busy all day."

"But thank heaven," said Blondel, "that this will probably be the only battle; we won't have to fight all over England."

The Captain nodded. "I wonder what Richard will do with him?"

"Nothing, probably." Blondel knew how Richard would treat his brother; knew, also, how he would like to treat him. "Exile, I suspect, and change the succession for good."

"I'd hate to be a king," said Karl, drawing a crown in the ashes.

"Do you think Richard will stay in England very long this time?" asked the Captain. A horse whinnied nearby and all three started, smiled sheepishly, relaxed with racing hearts.

"I don't think so; I expect he'll go back to France soon. He might even begin a new crusade. I don't know."

"He likes war," said the Captain, thoughtfully. "Most of us do, I think. It's very dull staying in one place, not traveling. I think men were made for it."

"It would seem so," said Blondel, not convinced.

"Well, I'd better see to the others." The Captain left them, creaking and clattering as he walked in his bright mail.

"How long do you think it's going to be?" asked Karl again.

"I don't know; do you have to keep asking?"

Some of the irritation and anger spilled over; Karl looked

hurt and, perversely, Blondel was pleased; he even scowled.

"I'm sorry. I didn't mean to bother you."

"Then don't keep asking questions." The damage was confirmed. Karl looked unhappily at the ashes and said nothing.

The sun was above the forest and it was dry. The wind still blew sharply in the trees and, in the west, rain clouds formed on the horizon. It would be clear for a few hours yet; no clouds in the sky directly overhead. Blondel stood up and walked over to his horse; without thinking he stretched and tested his muscles, in anticipation. The others were tense, too; no one spoke; they moved quietly now, arranging helmets, saddles.

Finally, high and clear, a horn sounded in the forest and Blondel mounted, calm at last, nerveless. The others mounted.

"Good luck," said Karl, smiling at him, touching the neck of his horse for a moment.

"Good luck," said Blondel and he tried to smile.

"Now!" shouted the captain. They followed him; Karl immediately behind him and Blondel farther back.

They rode down the hill and, as they did, they could see horsemen and archers coming out of the forest and down from the other hills.

The horn sounded again.

"Oh, God . . ." groaned Blondel, afraid, and he crossed himself as he rode towards Nottingham.

3

Sound mostly. Men shouting and screaming, some with pain. Horses neighing. Richard's voice rose occasionally over all the sound. The clanging of swords against shields, against helmets, armor; the whirring of arrows; chaotic sound.

And chaos in the battle itself. John's army met them before the gate. On the walls of the castle archers were posted, killing their own men in the field as well as the attackers. At times Blondel could hardly tell which men were Richard's and which John's. He fought only those who attacked him. He rode blindly, carried gradually toward the wall; he was a part, already, of the violence, the confusion.

He freed himself for a moment from the mass of men and iron and horses; he had been on the far flank and now, in an instant, he had been thrown out of the battle. He reined in his horse and stood up in his stirrups so that he could see. Hundreds of men were engaged before the wall; most of them mounted. Farther back, on a rise in the ground, Richard's archers took aim at the archers on the wall. The noise was terrible; he had forgotten all about the noise; he had forgotten how a scream sounded or the hiss of arrows and the hacking clang of metal on metal, sword against shield, sword against helmet. He squinted, tried to see Karl but could not; tried to find Richard and finally did. He was mounted on a black horse, conspicuous shouting and giving orders. There was always a path before him; few men would pause to fight with him and his sword often slashed air. His face was dark red, shining with sweat and, Blondel knew, though he was too far away actually to see, the veins in his temples stood out in pale knots. He could hear the voice, however; but no one could understand what he said. He shouted like an animal, harsh terrible sounds, spontaneous and natural.

The sun flashed on armor and arms, blinding flashes of light thrown off in all directions, glancing from the fighters like sparks from a giant forge. The sun was the hammer now; hot, hot and dazzlingly bright.

Something struck his shoulder and almost knocked him out of the saddle. An arrow had struck him, denting the metal scales. He looked up at the wall, at the towers, and wondered which man had tried to kill him. Then, rested, the design of the battle clear in his mind, he rode into the glittering confusion, into deafness.

He became a part of it. He could no longer distinguish the difference between a horse's scream and a man's, between the shout of triumph and the sound of a dying man. He kept his shield up; he was a careful fighter, not reckless like Richard, who would let his shield arm rest until the last possible moment. Blondel guarded himself and, when he attacked, fought deliberately.

The fear was gone. There was nothing in the world but this mass of men and horses gleaming in the hot sun. Ahead of him was a wall with a gate and, between the wall and the gate, both obscured by the fighting, there were a number of men whom he must either kill or wound. They succeeded one another regularly. As soon as one fell another took his place, and it seemed that he hardly moved. Yet move he did and he would reach the gate.

A tall knight: heavy lips and a thin face, an elaborately fashioned hauberk. The crash of the knight's sword on his shield. The hacking, the search for an opening. They were pressed side by side now; neither could withdraw to gain a new position or even to rest. They were pressed together, the knight's leg armor clanking against his own. Cover himself – now strike – his arm arched – cover himself again – a heavy blow. He almost lost his seat, almost fell. Then sword against sword, opening; now! quickly. Across the heavy lips a bar of red; the mouth dropped open and, with a look of surprise, the knight fell and was lost under the hoofs of horses.

Blondel rested his arms. He was pressed in tightly by

195

fighting men and riderless horses. He caught a glimpse of Karl, his face shiny and his mouth open, breathing hard or, perhaps, shouting, like the King. Some men shouted naturally when they fought.

He looked down for an instant and saw a man twisting and screaming under the hoofs of his horse. He looked up quickly, looked at the wall where fewer archers stood, looked at the sky where clouds were forming, thick and gray on the edge of the west. Then straight ahead; he looked for the next man, wondered which he would be, what his face would be like.

There was an open path of a few yards in front of him. Someone had fallen and there was a path: he rode into it before it closed. He was close to the wall now, close to the gate.

The next man had a blond beard, a yellow Saxon beard, and his skin was fair. He was a poorer knight, for his hauberk was made of bands of leather fastened with metal studs and it had already been torn, showing a patch of white above the breast. This was where he would strike, thought Blondel, and he looked, fascinated, at the white skin where his sword would go.

The man charged him as best he could with so few yards between them. The first blow stunned Blondel, glancing off his shield, striking his conical metal helmet. His eyes were dazzled as lights spun in his head. He kept his shield up, though, and, desperately, he shook his head until the light faded. The man had been thrown slightly off balance after his charge; he had been unable to attack again and he had lost his advantage.

They fought close to one another. Blondel could hear the other man's breathing, felt his breath in his face. The man was young, he saw, strong but inexperienced – as young as

Karl. Then, fulfilling prophecy, performing, in reality, a dream, he struck and the sword went into the white skin, sank deep and, quickly, was withdrawn. He looked away as the man fell, looked at the archers again. He heard a scream near him but it could have been anyone. When he looked again a riderless horse was in front of him and he could ride forward a few more yards.

He had never been so hot. The light tunic he wore under the hauberk was wet and clung clammily to him but he had no time to think of that; he noticed he was breathing in gasps, like a dog; he licked his lips: they were rough and tasted of salt.

Now another one, a Saxon, another Saxon. He put up his shield, defended himself against a series of blows; the Saxon was a cleverer, a better swordsman than he. He was too tired now to be afraid; he defended himself and waited. Then an opening came as two men fell at the same time, two already unhorsed men. He spurred his horse and escaped. He looked back and saw the opening had closed behind him. The Saxon was fighting another knight.

He was close to the wall now. John's men were falling back in an irregular line, defending every foot. He looked about him. Several men, ground soldiers, were fighting with broadswords and axes. Two knights fought close to him, shouting at one another. He caught a glimpse of Richard, closer to him than before; he rode a white horse now.

Blondel was thankful his own horse had survived and, as always when he congratulated himself, his horse stumbled and fell, an arrow through the neck. There was a crash and the earth shook and vibrated. Without thinking he clung to the horse, protecting himself behind its body. Finally, his head cleared and the earth ceased to vibrate. His leg hurt him; his ankle and foot were caught under the horse. He looked up and saw the bellies of horses and the spurred feet of knights. He clung to the animal while he tried to free his ankle. Hoofs narrowly missed him. He looked through the forest of horses' legs, found where the wall was, and grabbing his sword, freed his leg, got to his feet and ran to the wall. His ankle was badly hurt but he felt nothing while he ran. Breathless, he clung to the wall, safe for a time.

He had lost his helmet and his left hand was bleeding where it had hit the ground. He bound it with a piece of his tunic. He didn't look at his foot, tried not to think of it, tried to ignore the pain. He ran his good hand over his face and brushed the sweat and dust out of his eyes. The line of John's men was now broken in many places. He stood, fortunately, in one of the gaps. Several dead men lay near him as well as one wounded man who groaned and twisted. He looked at the dead, saw their wounds and how they died. Yet actually he noticed nothing; he would, he knew, forget everything when the battle ended.

He wondered where Karl was; he could see him nowhere. Then, not finding Karl, he looked for riderless horses. He saw several but he would have to run to catch them. Wearily he leaned against the wall, his weight on his good leg.

Richard appeared suddenly.

4

Richard waited restlessly in the forest for the sun to rise. He had arrived only the night before from Sandwich. He had been cheered in the towns through which he passed; he had recruited men and now, with a fair-sized though poorly organized army, he waited in the forest for morning.

William of l'Etoug was with him, kept him company while

he walked about the campfire or rustled his parchment map of Nottingham. Fires glittered at intervals all through the forest. Men wandered from camp to camp; in the distance, through the trees, he could see the lights of Nottingham across the meadows. A dozen boys sat near the fire, some sleeping, others awake and talking: they were messengers and each time he thought of some new detail of battle he would dispatch one of the boys to the captain concerned. The plan of battle was clear in his mind. He knew where each of his captains was; even the men down from London whom he hadn't yet seen. They had all been given their orders. The attack would come in two waves. The first shortly after dawn, and the second an hour later and from a different direction. He saw the design in his mind, saw it clearly as he usually did. He was excited. This was what he had missed most in the German prisons: to arrange a battle, to move the pieces about, to gamble, and, of course, to win. He flexed his arm; oh, to be rid of all this energy! to sleep until morning, to skip the intervening hours and the wasted time. The men who were still awake watched him as he moved nervously about. He knew that they were afraid of him and not merely because he was King; well, it was good to have them afraid, to have them call him Lion-Heart. He liked the sound of that.

The design of the battle filled his mind; everything else was excluded. So many men to the north, to the west, to the east; so many men in the forest, in the hills. Strange he had not heard from John; his own ambassador, the one he had sent John from Sandwich, had never returned. But tomorrow everyone would know. Tomorrow he would see John. The archers would take up their positions on the nearest hill. The cavalry would charge from the forest towards the gate . . .

"Someone to see you, Sir," said William, touching his arm.

"What? Who?" A man had stepped into the circle of fire-light. A short stocky man with a dark complexion and a dark beard; he wore a green tunic, much patched, and he carried a bow; he bowed with an incongruous elegance.

"King Richard?"

"Yes. Who are you? For us or for John?"

"For the King, Sir." Another bow, not quite so deep this time. "I'm Master Hood, an outlaw, a thief and, with your leave, Sir, the lord of this forest."

"Well, are you now!" Richard started to laugh, amused and a little shocked: was the man serious? would he dare joke like this?

"I have," said Master Hood serenely, "several hundred armed men who know not only the forest but Nottingham itself as well as their own faces: perhaps better, since they see their own faces less often. They're mostly archers, though all of them can use the broadsword. Can you use us?"

"Certainly. But at what price, Master Hood, at what price?"

"Whatever Your Majesty sees fit to give us."

"Diplomatic, aren't you?" Richard chuckled. "You'll have to be more exact than that. What are your terms?"

"Certain changes in the administration at Nottingham, inevitable changes, I suspect, and the repeal of several death sentences."

"You're quite right, Master Hood, that there will be a change in administration: I can assure you of that. As for the death sentences, I'll study them."

"I can ask no more," said Master Hood and he bowed again.

Gray light shone between the branches of the trees, birds sang and new leaves unfolded. The morning was cool and windless in the forest. A murmur of voices, of horses moving, of armor clattering: Richard had not slept at all. He and Master Hood had talked until the light broke.

As always, everything took longer than he had expected. He swore and shouted but delay he knew, was unavoidable, and the sun was already over the forest, yellow and bright, before they were ready to attack. Messengers rushed in and out of the clearing: orders to captains, messages from captains. He did everything himself. He could still see the design in his head.

When they were finally prepared, they mounted; everyone knew what to do. Several of his own captains mounted with him, ready to ride beside him. A young Saxon rode next to him, carrying the royal standard. William joined him, riding a chestnut horse. "I hear Blondel's on the hill, with the group from London."

"Oh, good; I've missed him." And he had. Blondel had been a valuable friend; but now to shape the battle. The moment began. "Sound the horn!" Then he gave the order to charge, using a language of his own which warriors always understood.

He galloped out of the forest, the standard-bearer beside him and William just behind. The sunlight was dazzling after the green darkness of the forest. He looked at the hills and saw the men charging, fulfilling the design.

Out of the forest a line of men galloped, following him towards Nottingham. Master Hood's archers, all dressed in green, appeared on the proper hill.

Now they would fight.

He was conscious of his own voice, of impatience as he shouted at his men, directed them towards weak parts of the enemy line. He stood high in his stirrups, judging the enemy's strength, the distribution of the men before the wall and the archers on the wall. Arrows shot about him but he knew he would not be touched; *he* couldn't die in battle. Now, sure of the field, he charged, shouting into the mass, his standard bearer behind him.

He no longer thought. Arm rising and falling, the familiar ring of metal on metal; smell of horses, sweat and dust and blood gleaming brightly on the dying and the dead. Few of John's men stayed to fight with him. A path opened for him whenever he tried to attack. They were afraid.

Then a baron, a man he had known and disliked, a vain foolish man, one of John's captains, stood in his way, made him stop.

"Fight, Richard!" the man cried. He fought, exhilarated, his sword arm rising, falling quickly, smashing and denting the other's shield. Never to stop! A final crash with his sword and the baron's helmet split and Richard's sword cut the foolish brain. "Fight, Richard!" the King mocked, as the baron, dead, fell from his horse, vanished under the battle.

Moving and cutting and shouting, watching the line of the enemy, watching the ramparts, watching the hills behind him: soon, now, soon. All the humiliation of two years in prison, of two years' inactivity was forgotten, purged, lost in noise, in the blood-dappled dust of Nottingham.

Faces, one after another, staring at him under acorn-like helmets, watching him: red faces, shiny faces, all watching him, a circle of faces and all afraid. An oval face, plump and soft with a short beard: two blows and the plump oval sank in a sea of horses. He would never see that face again. An arrow glanced off his helmet. Furious, he attacked a swarthy face, a frightened face, and made it bleed for the sake of an archer who had dared try to kill him, to kill *him*.

He charged and then, in a moment (only a moment? timeless battle, endless violence, motion, and his own voice coming up from his chest) or, at least, soon in this place of static violence, he found himself at the wall and there, leaning against it, was Blondel.

He reined in his horse close to the wall, protected by a pediment from anything the defenders might want to drop on him. John's men were retreating through the gate. He shouted to William to press after them, to get through the gate if possible. William understood. He attacked.

"Are you hurt?"

Blondel nodded, pointing to his ankle. Richard was aware that his own voice had cracked, that his throat felt raw. "Bad?"

Blondel shook his head. There was dust on his face and a splatter of blood across the shoulder of his armor. "We've waited a long time," he said, barely able to make himself heard.

Richard felt suddenly gentle, warm, oblivious, for a moment, of the battle. "I won't forget," he said, looking at Blondel, who looked away. Why did people never look directly at him? why would no one look at him? even Blondel avoided his eyes. "I'll get you a horse." He shouted to his standard-bearer, who trotted out from the shelter of the wall, was almost hit by a falling boulder, secured a riderless horse and, in a few minutes, was back. Blondel mounted. "Almost over," said Richard; then he returned to battle.

At first Karl was bewildered. The noise hurt his eardrums; the bright sun reflected over and over again in armor dazzled his eyes and made him blink. He was lost without Blondel, directionless. He rode uncertainly after the captain and his company. At first they trotted down the rocky hill; then, when they came to the large meadow, they galloped.

This was more what he had expected. It was exciting to feel his horse lunging under him. The fighting closed about him and he was lost. Which were the enemy? Many solved this problem by shouting "For Richard!" and if someone shouted back "For John!" they fought. He tried this and found many of the enemy.

He got used to the rhythm of attack and defend. He was strong, he knew, stronger than most of these knights who had experienced many battles, had studied and mastered the business of fighting. His strength made up for his lack of experience.

He had killed several men before he realized what was happening, what he had done. He had smashed one fellow's arm and, as the man ducked away from him, leaving him for an instant in command of an open place in the battle, he realized what he was doing and he was shocked and a little proud. He had wanted all of this: violence and confused movement, but in actuality it was different from anything he had expected. He had never imagined anything like this: the succession of mounted knights in his way each trying to kill him and he trying to kill each of them. Then the absence of a visible plan disturbed and confused him. He knew they had to take the wall in front of him but he had no idea how it was to be done, no idea what was expected of him other than to move forward and avoid being killed. So he rode towards the wall. He was stopped again and he fought again.

Better not to think; in fact, impossible to think, to consider now. He was being pushed forward by the force of an army behind him and he was resisted by an army in front of him. He was the center of the world of men and horses, and over everything the sun burned; the heat from his own body escaped in a hot gust from the neck of his hauberk. He could feel sweat streaming down his face, blinding him with salt, wetting his dry lips.

The battle turned to one side. The force that had pushed him straight forward hit him obliquely now, threw him with a group of men, no more than twenty of them, off to one edge of the battle, to the edge of the meadow farthest from the wall. Free for a second, he watched the men moving upon the wall and the thinning line of defenders. Riderless horses moved aimlessly over the meadow, outside the fighting. He could see a standard being raised beside the wall and, near it, a tall, shouting man with a red-brown beard: so that was Richard. He squinted in the bright sun to see him better but, as he squinted, both standard and King disappeared, lost in the brilliant shifting mass.

He wiped his face with the back of his sword hand. His hands were trembling, he noticed; his whole body trembled: not fear but tension. Now which way? To the wall again obviously, that was the proper direction. But first he must move beyond the nearest group of men: a cluster of mounted knights fighting, Richard's men outnumbered by those of John.

He spurred his horse.

Dark eyebrows meeting and a thin mouth: they fought.

He was stronger but for the first time he realized his own inexperience. He hammered and slashed out but the knight's shield took each blow. He grew furious and he swore. He hated the thin mouth. For the first time in his life he hated.

His arm moved without tiring, muscles tensed and relaxed regularly. He reined his horse this way and that and, when defending himself, he even guided the animal with his knees; but he couldn't get beyond the shield, couldn't shatter the shield and destroy the man.

205

He knew, while he repeated his attacks, that the other was waiting for him to tire, to drop his shield; well, he wouldn't tire. A stroke. A shattering sound and sparks under the sun. Again.

Then, like a bad dream, he saw two more knights riding towards him. He reined in his horse, turned and tried to escape but they stopped him, blocked his way.

There was nothing to do. No escape. The three closed in, slowly, deliberately. He defended himself, fought back, silently, his body like ice and his lips trembling.

Fire touched his shoulder. His sword fell from his hands. A shout from one of the men and then a heavy blow against his chest. He fell.

He opened his eyes and saw the sun like a shield of brass. He turned his head and saw the knight with the thin mouth riding towards him. Was he going to help him? Then suddenly he knew what was going to happen. He screamed but the mass of white was over him, the unicorn was riderless and the sun gone.

THE ENVOI

Blondel did not find him until twilight. The battle was over and Richard had taken Nottingham. Not finding Karl in the town, Blondel left Richard and walked alone in the meadows before the wall.

Dead men and dead horses were everywhere: now in a tangled group where fighting had been particularly fierce; now separate, at a distance from one another. Officers of both sides walked among the dead, identifying them, making the count. Now and then a figure stirred; a man called out or groaned. Most of the wounded had been collected, however. Those left here were, almost all of them, dead or dying.

He walked, sick and tired among them, recognizing a few. Villagers, scavengers, were already at work, robbing and stripping the bodies.

The twilight was cool, a relief after the heat. He had discarded his hauberk and changed his tunic. A light wind blew and overhead clouds filled the sky and, in the distance, lightning flashed; soon it would storm and, anticipating this, he pulled his cloak tight.

He would not worry about Karl. Instead he imagined John's meeting with Richard; or had John fled? No one

207

knew yet. They were still searching the castle but John's army was broken to pieces. What little was left of it had already sworn allegiance to the King and, soon, they would be back in London and then to France: the three of them.

Richard, triumphant again, had been a moving sight. His voice had gone shortly before the battle ended. Whispering, he had received the surrendering captains. He had made a speech, though.

"There's been some talk," he had said, careful to keep his voice from cracking, looking at the captains, barons and knights, all dirt-stained, standing before him in the great hall of Nottingham Castle. "There has been talk that I accepted the Emperor as my overlord, as a condition of my release. Therefore let us say," and he fingered a proclamation which would be given to all England, "that what promises we might have made to the Holy Roman Emperor," he mocked the title as he spoke it, "were never binding since we were held illegally captive when we made them. And, further, if there is any doubt in the minds of our English barons as to who is King we shall dispel it just as we dispelled the army of our brother John today. And, finally, as a sign to our English barons and to the Emperor and to all the Christian princes, we command you to attend us at our cathedral at Winchester where, within the week, we will wear the crown." He had stopped then, his voice gone. The men had cheered him and he had looked back at them grinning, assured and solitary.

Blondel had left after this. The surgeon bound his foot, which was bruised but not seriously damaged. Then, not seeing Karl, he went to look for him. He walked slowly across the battlefield.

At the edge of the meadow, several yards from the nearest trace of battle, he found Karl. The boy lay on his back, his legs crossed, one arm thrown back and the other over his face, protectively. The scavengers had found him earlier: his helmet, his weapons, his shoes and his cloak were gone; they had left only the torn hauberk on him. His skin was dull and white and smeared with drying blood.

Blondel stood over him, wondering what he should do, what he should feel. All the noise and violence of the day had used up his energy and his emotions, destroyed all power to act and to believe. He stood looking at the boy; then slowly, he got down beside him and lifted Karl's arm out of his face. The face was pale and the bright hair full of blood: there was no expression, no sign of fear or pain.

Blondel put the head in his lap. A cold rain fell, an early spring rain, but he was not aware of it. He remained a long time. It had ended; his own youth lay dead in the rain and he would be old now, unprotected, centered in himself and never young again. The wind, shrill-sounding, full of rain, raked the meadow, blew through Sherwood Forest. The twilight, thick with rain clouds, was almost as dark as night.

A man came walking across the meadow, walking alone, aware of the dead about him, stooping from time to time to look at faces, to recognize the unfamiliar faces of dead friends. Blondel watched without interest, recognizing, finally, the King.

"You found him," Richard whispered, his voice unexpectedly weak.

Blondel said nothing.

"He's dead," said Richard, kneeling, touching the boy's face. Then Richard helped Blondel to his feet.

"I'll see he's buried here," said the King. "Now we must go." In darkness they crossed the meadow towards the town of Nottingham and the victory feast.

☐ Creation	Gore Vidal	£5.99
☐ Duluth	Gore Vidal	£5.99
☐ Julian	Gore Vidal	£5.99
☐ Kalki	Gore Vidal	£5.99
☐ Live from Golgotha	Gore Vidal	£5.99
☐ Messiah	Gore Vidal	£5.99
☐ Myra Breckinridge & Myron	Gore Vidal	£6.99
☐ Screening History	Gore Vidal	£5.99
☐ A View from the Diners Club	Gore Vidal	£5.99

Abacus now offers an exciting range of quality titles by both established and new authors. All of the books in this series are available from:

Little, Brown and Company (UK) Limited,
P.O. Box 11,
Falmouth,
Cornwall TR10 9EN.

Alternatively you may fax your order to the above address. Fax No. 0326 376423.

Payments can be made as follows: cheque, postal order (payable to Little, Brown and Company) or by credit cards, Visa/Access. Do not send cash or currency. UK customers and B.F.P.O. please allow £1.00 for postage and packing for the first book, plus 50p for the second book, plus 30p for each additional book up to a maximum charge of £3.00 (7 books plus).

Overseas customers including Ireland, please allow £2.00 for the first book plus £1.00 for the second book, plus 50p for each additional book.

NAME (Block Letters) ....

....

ADDRESS ....

....

....

☐ I enclose my remittance for _____

☐ I wish to pay by Access/Visa Card

Number ☐☐☐☐☐☐☐☐☐☐☐☐☐☐☐☐

Card Expiry Date ☐☐☐☐